Ghost Train

For my nieces and my nephew:

Delphine   Isabella

Sophie   Nicky

Nicolas   Catherine

—A. C.

A Peachtree Junior Publication

Published by
PEACHTREE PUBLISHERS
1700 Chattahoochee Avenue
Atlanta, Georgia 30318-2112

www.peachtree-online.com

Text © 2004 by Anne Capeci
Illustrations © 2004 by Paul Casale

Book design by Loraine M. Joyner
Composition by Melanie McMahon Ives

Photographs pages 125-126, 131-132 from the author's family collection; photograph page 130 courtesy of the Library of Congress; poster page 32 courtesy of Kansas State Historical Society; illustrations pages i-viii, 129, 131-132 by Paul Casale.

Manufactured in China
10 9 8 7 6 5 4 3 2 1
First Edition

Library of Congress Cataloging-in-Publication Data

Capeci, Anne.
   Ghost train / written by Anne Capeci ; illustrated by Paul Casale.-- 1st ed.
     p. cm. -- (The Cascade Mountain railroad mysteries ; no. 3)
   Includes bibliographical references and index.
   Summary: When Billy finds a burlap sack containing a pistol and a cryptic, threatening note, he and his best friends Dannie and Finn set out to learn who holds a grudge and is plotting against the railroad.
   ISBN 1-56145-324-2
   [1. Railroads--Trains--Fiction. 2. Robbers and outlaws--Fiction. 3. Pageants--Fiction. 4. Northwest, Pacific--History--20th century--Fiction. 5. Mystery and detective stories.] I. Casale, Paul, ill. II. Title.

PZ7.C17363Gh 2004
   [Fic]--dc22   2004009179

CASCADE MOUNTAIN
3
RAILROAD MYSTERIES

Ghost Train

ANNE CAPECI

PEACHTREE
ATLANTA

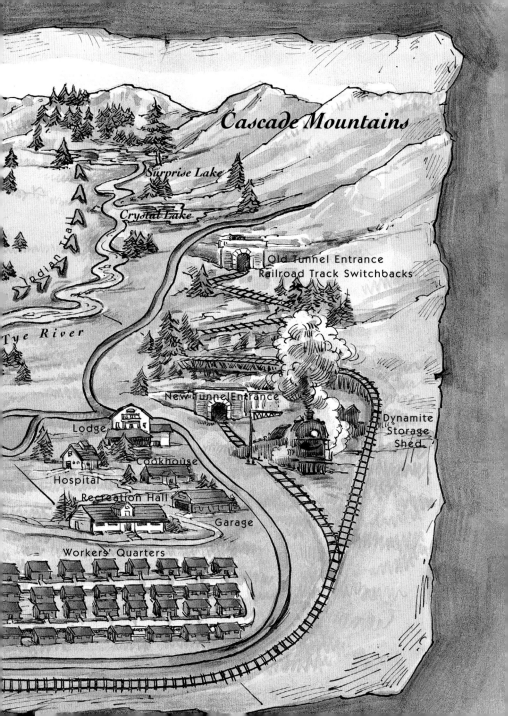

Acknowledgments

The author would like to thank the following people for their invaluable help in researching and preparing this book: David Conroy, Margaret Conroy Capeci, and Elizabeth (Buffy) Rempel for the wonderful stories and memories that made this series possible; Pete Conroy, for generously allowing the use of his photographs; Eva Anderson, author of *Rails Across the Cascades,* which provided wonderful historical information; Lisa Banim, for her expert guidance in helping to shape the story; the Great Northern Railway Historical Society, for helping me to find detailed information about how the Cascade Tunnel was built; and HistoryLink.org and the National Library of Canada, for information about silk trains.

Table of Contents

Chapter 1:   Sneak Attack. 1

Chapter 2:   Run!. 9

Chapter 3:   Ghost Train 15

Chapter 4:   A Secret Message 25

Chapter 5:   Unfair!. 33

Chapter 6:   Angry Words 43

Chapter 7:   Spoiled Plans 51

Chapter 8:   Gunshot on the Mountain. 59

Chapter 9:   Grizzly!. 63

Chapter 10: Chasing Trouble 73

Chapter 11: A Sneaky Plan. 83

Chapter 12: Following Clues 89

Chapter 13: Signal From Seattle. 99

Chapter 14: Too Late! 107

Chapter 15: No Time to Lose 115

Author's Note 125

Chapter One

SNEAK ATTACK

Scenic, Washington
1926

ook out below!" shouted Billy Cole.

He grabbed the rope that hung from a tree at the edge of the Tye River. A deep pool had formed there, in a bend in the river.

Billy and the other children who lived in Scenic had spent the whole day in the deliciously cold water. Even now, with supper eaten and the sun low in the sky, a handful of boys and girls had returned in their damp woolen bathing suits for one last dunk.

And maybe for a prank, too, Billy thought.

Holding on tight to the rope, he leaped from the riverbank. A thrill shot through him as he swung out over the water. The final golden rays of sun shone on the Cascade Mountains overhead and the air smelled richly of pine. In a dizzy flash, Billy saw the wood-frame buildings of the work camp through the trees.

Billy and his family had lived in Scenic ever since work on the new railroad tunnel had begun. The tunnel itself was out of sight, on the far side of camp. But Billy could hear the faint sounds of dynamite blasting, and of pumps and drills and work engines.

As he reached the peak of his swing, a girl's voice made Billy look down. *Perfect,* he thought. Alice Ann Lockhart, the biggest know-it-all in Scenic, was swimming just below him.

"I've already learned my lines for the Fourth of July pageant," Billy heard Alice Ann jabber to her friends Lucy and Janet. "Betsy Ross is one of the most important roles, you know."

She paddled carefully, keeping her chin-length blond hair out of the water. In her brand-new, blue-and-white-striped bathing costume, she looked as perfect as a china doll.

Not for long, Billy thought.

He let go of the rope and dropped into the river. Then he kicked wildly with his arms and legs, splashing water all around.

"Stop it!" Alice Ann sputtered. But it was too late.

Her hair was soaking wet and plastered to her cheeks. Billy had to choke back a laugh.

"Gee, did I do that?" he asked in his most innocent voice.

"You know you did!" Alice Ann shot back. She climbed out of the water and sat on the riverbank in a huff. Water dripped from her suit onto the layer of pine needles on the ground. "You're just jealous 'cause I'm in the pageant and you're not!"

"Well, you got me there, Alice Ann," Billy said. He kicked lazily across the swimming hole. "Here Finn and Dannie and me are stuck having fun and doing any old thing we want all day long. It's just terrible!"

Laughter rang out from above the swimming hole. Billy's best pals, Finn Mackenzie and Dannie Renwick, stood on the bank. Red-haired Finn was just reaching for the rope Billy had abandoned. His eyes sparkled with fun.

"That's right," Finn said. "I'd much rather be cooped up in the schoolhouse learning lines and pretending to be folks who've been dead for over a hundred years."

"Besides, anyone can be in the pageant who wants to," Dannie added. She tugged at the ill-fitting bathing suit that had been handed down to her by her brother.

Her dog, Buster, was next to her. "Your mother's already been to the cabin three times to ask me, Alice Ann. I just don't want to, that's all."

Lucy and Janet were still swimming near Billy. He saw the disapproving way they stared at Dannie.

"Well," said Janet, "if you don't want to celebrate the one hundred and fiftieth birthday of our country, I guess that's your business."

"Oh, I'll celebrate," Dannie said. "In my own way."

With that, she took a running jump and splashed into the river. Finn dropped from the swinging rope a moment later. Buster barked while the two of them splashed and dunked with Billy. Their wild play sent Lucy and Janet diving away. Glaring, the girls climbed out of the water to join Alice Ann.

That left just Philip Mackey in the river with Billy, Dannie, and Finn. Philip leaned against a rock at the edge of the swimming hole, in shallow water up to his waist.

"Father made me join the pageant," Philip said. His straight hair had fallen over his eyes. Brushing it back, he glanced up at Alice Ann. His face turned bright red, and he looked quickly away again. "But I guess it's not so bad," he mumbled.

Billy had to roll his eyes. He got along fine with

Philip most times. But for some reason, the railroad owner's son was always trying to impress Alice Ann. For the life of him, Billy couldn't understand why.

"I'll tell you one thing. The Fourth of July pageant is a whole lot more fun than some dumb pretend war," Alice Ann said. She looked over at Billy, Finn, and Dannie. "Especially when *your* side doesn't stand a chance."

She, Lucy, and Janet all started giggling. Billy felt his cheeks burn.

"You take that back!" he said. But he knew he didn't sound convincing. He and Dannie and Finn had been beaten by the other "army" in every battle so far.

The "war" had begun just two weeks earlier, on the day classes in Scenic's two-room schoolhouse had ended for the summer. Wes and Eddie Gundy, along with Eddie's friend Jim Walsh, had attacked them with pinecones as they left the school yard. Since then, the two "armies" had been going after each other with pinecones, pails of water, and any other "ammunition" they could find.

"It's not our fault Eddie and Jim are bigger than us," Finn grumbled. "They're two grades ahead at school."

"And Wes tries to act bigger, even though he's ten, like us," Dannie added.

Billy quickly peered into the trees on either side of the river. How could he have forgotten to be on the alert for an attack?

Reluctantly he dragged out of the water. Darkness was beginning to settle over the woods. Trees and rocks and scurrying squirrels were melting into a tangle of shadows. Suddenly Billy thought he saw something move.

"That's Wes's red cap!" he whispered.

"Where?" Alice Ann said loudly.

"*Shh!*" Dannie told her.

Billy squinted hard at the spot in the trees. Sure enough, Wes was peeking out from behind a Douglas fir tree. Billy didn't see Eddie or Jim. But he had a feeling they were nearby.

"It's them, all right," he whispered.

Quickly he bent to pick up some pinecones. Finn and Dannie clambered out of the water and did the same. As Billy reached for more cones, Buster hustled in front of him. The retriever crouched over his front paws. He sniffed at some wasps that circled the low branches of a fir tree.

"Wasps, eh?" Billy murmured.

He tilted his head back and stared up higher into the tree. There, about a dozen feet up, hung a wasps' nest.

The paper-like ball was pale against the dark, bushy branches. It was as big as a melon, Billy guessed. Maybe even bigger.

Then an idea popped into Billy's head. "We might beat the Gundys and Jim Walsh yet," he whispered.

Dannie saw the nest, too. "Sure," she said. "All we've got to do is knock it out of the tree at exactly the right moment."

"Knock *what* out of the tree?" Alice Ann asked.

Billy opened his mouth to tell her to clear out of the way. But he never got the words out. At that moment, Wes, Eddie, and Jim burst from the trees. They were shouting like banshees and throwing something Billy couldn't see clearly.

Sticks and pinecones rained down on Billy's head and shoulders. Lucy, Janet, and Alice Ann jumped up, their shrieks filling the air. Buster seemed to be everywhere at once, barking.

Somehow Billy got his hand around a rock. He heaved it up at the wasps' nest. He heard a thud and saw the nest hit the ground.

Right next to Alice Ann, Lucy, and Janet.

Chapter Two

RUN!

Alice Ann screamed.

The next thing Billy knew, wasps were everywhere. A huge, angry, buzzing cloud of them. He felt a sting on his arm, then another on his neck.

"Ow!" yelled Dannie, swatting wasps away from her legs. "Run!"

The girls' shrieks were even louder now. Billy heard a splash as someone leaped into the water. Feet thumped away through the trees, snapping branches as they went.

"Come on, Billy!" Dannie yelled. She and Finn charged past him.

Billy took off behind them. The stings on his neck and arm hurt like crazy. His wet woolen suit was itchy and cold. All he could think about was getting away from the wasps. He ran blindly, aware only of Dannie's pale arms and legs pumping away in front of him. He didn't stop to think about where he was. Until he felt sharp pieces of gravel digging into the soles of his bare feet.

"H-hold up!" he said, doubling over to catch his breath.

He blinked, surprised. How had they gotten all the way across camp? They were three-quarters of the way along the gravel road that curved around Scenic. The cookhouse, recreation hall, hospital, and old lodge were already behind them. The family cabins where they lived were so far back that Billy couldn't even see them.

"Finn? Dannie?" Billy frowned, peering ahead. "Hey! Wait up!"

His friends hadn't stopped. The two of them had moved onto the train tracks that ran alongside the road. They hurried along the rails in their bare feet and swimsuits. Buster trotted on the ground next to them.

Ahead of them was the new tunnel. Electric lights were strung across the thick beams that framed the entrance. They sent a yellow glow over the chunks of granite that were piled high nearby. Billy had climbed onto the blasted rock countless times to search for garnets. Every so often he found one of the purplish brown crystals embedded in a rock. He kept them stowed away in a cigar box under his bed at home.

But Dannie and Finn weren't looking for garnets. They had run past the rails that branched off toward the tunnel. Beyond, there was nothing but the dark, empty mountainside.

"Come on!" Dannie called over her shoulder to Billy. "We're going to the snow sheds!"

"Wait for me!" Billy called back. He hurried to catch up to his friends. The railway tracks gleamed faintly in the dying sunshine, rising up the dark mountainside. Billy had to blink a few times before he could make out the sloping roof of the snow shed that covered the tracks about fifty feet ahead.

The sheds had been built to protect trains during the winter. Every child in Scenic had heard stories of avalanches—big snow slides that destroyed everything in their paths. The worst had taken place in Wellington, a tiny town higher up the mountain. An avalanche had slammed into two trains, sending them crashing down the mountainside. Over a hundred people died. That was why the snow sheds were built to cover long stretches of track. Snow rolled right over the sheds without disturbing any trains beneath.

Of course, the snow was long gone now. Boys and girls found other uses for the sheds during the summer.

They played and ran races inside them all the time. Still, Billy felt himself hesitate.

"What if a train comes?" he yelled up to Dannie.

Dannie kept right on going. "The local came through an hour ago," she called back. "There won't be another one 'til morning."

"Besides, we'd better keep clear of our cabins for awhile," Finn added. "I bet Wes and Eddie and Jim are just waiting for another chance to attack us. And Alice Ann is probably blabbing to anyone who will listen about how we knocked that wasps' nest out of the tree."

If Billy had to choose between the pitch-black snow shed or going home to face his angry parents, he knew right away what his decision was.

He sprinted past his friends. "Race you to the other end!" he shouted. "Come on, you slow-pokes!"

"No fair! You got a head start!" Finn shouted. But he and Dannie were both laughing. Billy heard their feet slap against the railroad ties behind him. Buster's barking echoed in the growing darkness.

Billy ran underneath the snow shed roof. Right away the air felt cooler. The damp fog seemed to close around him.

"I'll...catch...you...yet, Billy!" Dannie puffed. Billy felt as if his chest would burst from running so fast.

Buster was barking louder than ever in the closed-in space. The sound echoed in Billy's ears, and at first he didn't notice the deep rumbling beneath his feet.

"H-huh?" Billy slowed his pace. There was only one thing that made the tracks shake like that. He glanced behind him—and gasped.

"A train!" he cried. "It's heading straight for us!"

Chapter Three
GHOST TRAIN

Billy's breath froze inside his chest. "Train!" he yelled again.

Finn and Dannie didn't seem to hear him. They were still racing toward him on the tracks, and the train was coming up fast behind them.

"Get off...*now!*" Billy tried to push his friends off the tracks, but they were going too fast. They smashed into him. The three of them fell to the tracks in a heap.

Only then did Finn and Dannie hear the chugging engine. Its powerful beam cut through the fog behind them.

"No!" Finn cried, his eyes popping wide. He scrambled to untangle himself from Dannie and Billy. Buster grabbed Dannie's bathing suit in his muzzle, pulling her toward the edge of the tracks. Billy stumbled after them, trying to find his footing.

We'll never make it! Billy thought. The train was already charging beneath the snow shed. It was almost on top of them!

The train's whistle pierced the night air. Billy pushed hard with his feet and dived headfirst from the tracks.

A split second later, the engine roared past and hot air blasted over Billy's head. By the time he got his feet underneath him again, the train was past.

"F-Finn? Dannie?" he called.

Two figures pushed themselves up from the rocks and brush that sloped down from the tracks. "We're here," Dannie said. Buster gave her cheek a lick.

"What *was* that?" Finn said. He picked his way up the slope toward Billy.

The train was traveling farther up the mountain now. Billy could make out the boxy shapes of half a dozen railcars. But there was something strange about them. Not a single light shone in the cars. The chugging train looked dark and sinister in the mist.

"Don't know," Billy said. He tried to shake off the uneasy feeling that had come over him. "The last local came through already, like Dannie said. And the *North - ern Express* from Seattle isn't due 'til morning." He frowned, picking at the pine needles and twigs that had stuck to his damp bathing suit. "What kind of a train doesn't have lights on the cars?"

"A ghost train?" Finn said in a shaky voice.

"It nearly flattened us like griddle cakes! No ghost could do that," Dannie said. She climbed up to the tracks and sat on the outside rail. "I bet it was just a freight train. One that's not on the schedule."

Billy frowned. *Every train follows a schedule,* he thought. The timetable was posted at the depot for everyone to see. But all he said was, "Let's go home. I don't want to run any more races."

This time Dannie and Finn didn't argue. Instead of retracing their steps along the rails, they cut down the hillside toward camp. It was a steeper but shorter route. In no time at all they reached the last fir trees before the road. Billy pushed past the bushy branches—and ran smack into someone coming the other way.

"Jeepers!" Billy leaped back. "Oh—it's you, Mr. Woods."

Trevor Woods was the telegraph operator at the Scenic camp. He worked downstairs from Billy's father's office in the old lodge. Billy had seen him around camp delivering telegrams, always moving with a quick step, as if he couldn't ever get where he was going fast enough.

"Well now!" Mr. Woods said, smiling broadly. He was a young man with slicked-back blond hair and a round face. "If you three are looking for the swimming hole, you sure are in the wrong place."

"We know where the swimming hole is, Mr. Woods. We went there before we came up here to play in the snow sheds," Dannie told him.

The young man's smile disappeared. "You were on the tracks? With that train coming through? You could have been killed!"

"It came out of nowhere!" said Finn. "What train was it, Mr. Woods?"

The train's beam was higher on the mountainside now. Mr. Woods watched it intently, then shook his head.

"Don't know," he answered. "I guess there's always something new coming along. New trains, new tunnels. Something bigger and better all the time. It's called progress, kids."

Billy shot a puzzled glance at Finn. What did progress have to do with a train nearly ramming them flat? "Um, yes sir," he said politely. "So no one sent word that it was coming?"

"Nope." Mr. Woods shook his head again. "I guess the fellas at the Seattle yards might have tried to wire me about it. The line's down. I'm tracking down the break right now, as a matter of fact."

He pointed at the telegraph wire overhead. It looped between tall poles set into the ground. Billy could barely see the wire through the mist. But sounds traveled clearly through the foggy, pine-scented air. In the distance Billy heard the sharp cry of an owl, the grinding of machines inside the tunnel, and the cheering of men at a boxing match in the recreation hall.

Then he heard something else. Voices speaking somewhere nearby. They sounded like boys' voices, not men's. And Billy knew exactly which boys they belonged to.

"Hear that?" he whispered to Dannie and Finn. "It's Wes and Eddie and Jim. I bet anything!"

"They must be looking for us," Dannie said. "Well, this time we'll give *them* a surprise attack they won't forget!" She began to gather up pinecones from the ground. "Bye, Mr. Woods!"

Billy heard the telegraph operator chuckle behind them. But as he darted toward the road, he couldn't stop thinking about the mysterious train. It had seemed so dark and threatening. Every time Billy pictured it in his mind, he shivered.

Finn, Dannie, and Billy crept toward the back of the cookhouse, in the shadow of the raised wooden walkway. Walkways ran between all the buildings at the center of camp. They made it easier to get around when there was snow or mud. Crouching underneath the boards, Finn pointed at a pair of fir trees behind the cookhouse.

"There!" Finn whispered.

Three people stood next to the trees. Billy recognized the stocky silhouettes of Wes and Eddie Gundy. Jim's taller, thinner figure was there, too. Billy was glad to see that the three boys had their backs to the cookhouse. They didn't seem to realize anyone else was nearby.

"Who cares, we'll never find them," Billy heard Wes say. He sounded tired. "Let's go home. Uncle Colin promised to shoot marbles with me tonight."

"Don't be such a baby," Eddie Gundy's deeper voice said. "Uncle Colin's not going back to Seattle 'til day after tomorrow. You can play marbles with him in the morning."

"Anyhow, don't you want to win the war?" Jim added.

Billy wasn't surprised by the older boys' bossy tones. Eddie and Jim were always picking on kids and telling them what to do. Listening to them, Billy wanted more than ever to beat them in the war.

Finn nudged Billy and Dannie, then counted silently on his fingers. One...two...three!

Billy, Finn, and Dannie dashed out from under the walkway. Billy gave a loud shout, hurling pinecones. All three of the boys jumped. They whirled around in startled surprise.

"What...?" cried Eddie.

"Take that!" Dannie shouted. She and Billy and Finn fired one pinecone after another. Buster jumped around them, barking excitedly. Sticks and pinecones flew so thickly toward the enemy that they could only stand with their arms over their heads. Billy and his friends kept up the attack until their supply ran out.

Only then did Billy see the angry glint in Eddie Gundy's eyes.

"Run!" Finn cried.

Billy didn't need to be told twice. He sprinted left, toward the hospital. He glanced over his shoulder. He didn't see Finn or Dannie. But Eddie was hot on his trail.

"Try and catch me!" Billy taunted. He thumbed his nose at Eddie and ran even faster.

Sure, Eddie was bigger than he was. But Eddie's stocky build slowed him down. He was still twenty feet back when Billy raced around the hospital. The lodge was just beyond. Billy ducked under the front steps.

Eddie came huffing around the hospital a moment later. He looked left, then right. An electric bulb over the hospital door lit up his puzzled frown.

Chuckling softly, Billy inched farther beneath the steps. There was a crawlspace underneath the lodge. It was only about three feet high, but that was enough. Crouching low, Billy ducked into the space.

He worked his way toward the other side of the lodge in the darkness. The ground was damp and smelled of mold. Twice Billy felt his wool bathing suit catch on rough wooden beams that supported the lodge.

Just a little way to the other side, he thought.

At last he saw a strip of paler gray ahead. Moonlight shining behind the lodge made the air brighter there. Billy crawled toward the spot—then frowned as his bare knee hit something hard.

He reached down and felt a dry burlap sack. There was a heavy clank of metal inside.

"Hmm," he murmured. Maybe he had discovered a bag of money!

As quietly as he could, he dragged the sack the last few feet to the back of the lodge. He glanced quickly outside, then crawled out into the open air.

Eddie was nowhere in sight.

Billy opened the sack and peered into it.

"Cripes!" he said softly.

Moonlight glinted off the metal barrel of a pistol.

Shiny bullets were piled around it. The sight of them made Billy's heart pound.

Slowly he reached inside the sack. A folded paper stuck out from among the bullets. As his fingers closed around it, he heard the soft scrape of feet on the pine needles behind him.

Before he could turn around, he felt something being pulled roughly over his head.

"Hey!" Billy cried. He dropped the bag with the pistol and yanked at the scratchy burlap of another sack. He couldn't get out from under it! Strong hands pulled the fabric tightly over his face.

He could hardly breathe!

Chapter Four
A SECRET MESSAGE

Help!" Billy yelled.

At least, he tried to. The burlap sack muffled his cry.

Two hands shoved hard into Billy's back. He stumbled forward onto his hands and knees and rolled over on the ground, twisting and pulling at the sack. It seemed like forever before he managed to get it off.

Throwing the bag aside, he jumped to his feet. He heard footsteps behind him.

"Finn! Dannie!" Billy said in relief as his friends came running out of the shadows. Buster tore ahead of Dannie, his tail wagging.

"We got away! We did it!" Finn said gleefully. He grinned from ear to ear—until he took a close look at Billy. "Gee whiz! What's the matter? Did Eddie catch you?" he asked.

"I—I don't know," Billy said. He glanced nervously around. "I...thought I lost him. Then I found a sack. It had a pistol in it. A real one! And then someone came up behind me and—"

"Pistol? What are you talking about?" Dannie interrupted. She pointed at the burlap sack that lay crumpled on the ground. "Where'd *that* come from?"

"That's what I'm trying to tell you!" Billy said.

"Billy Cole! Will you please start making sense?" Dannie exclaimed.

As quickly as he could, Billy told them what had happened. Finn and Dannie listened, their eyes growing wider and wider.

"I guess whoever it was took the pistol," Billy finished. "I sure don't see it now."

Dannie scanned the ground around them. "You could have been hurt!" she said. "You didn't see who did it?"

"Nope. He made sure I didn't see him," Billy said. "Whoever it was sure didn't want me to have that pistol."

"What about Wes and Eddie and Jim?" said Dannie.

Billy shook his head. "I doubt it," he said. "They weren't carrying any sacks. Anyhow, whoever pushed me felt bigger and stronger than a kid."

"What's that, Billy?" Finn said excitedly. He nodded at the folded sheet still clutched in Billy's hand.

Billy unfolded the paper. He held it out so it caught the moonlight. Three lines of words in messy handwriting read:

ELECTRIC STORM NOT ON SCHEDULE
WAIT FOR MY SIGNAL
THE GOAT WILL PAY

Finn stared at the words. "Well, that doesn't make any sense at all!"

"Maybe it's a code," Dannie suggested. "Whenever Papa talks about the railroad company, he calls it the Iron Goat."

"That's right," said Billy. Every kid in Scenic knew the goat was the symbol of the Great Northern Railway. Important men in the company were always bragging about how their trains could climb mountains as easily as nimble-footed goats. But knowing that didn't help him understand the message any better.

"'Electric storm not on schedule,'" he read out loud. "Do you think that's a code, too?"

"Beats me," said Finn. He pointed at the second line of the note. "And what's this about a signal? Sounds like there's some kind of secret plan."

"A plan to make the railway pay?" Dannie said, frowning. "Pay for what?"

Billy wasn't sure. But he didn't like the sound of it.

"Maybe it has something to do with the train that just came through," he said slowly. "That sure wasn't on any schedule. At least, I don't *think* it was."

"Let's go ask at the depot!" Finn said. Even in the darkness, his eyes gleamed with determination.

The Scenic depot was just a platform by the tracks next to the lodge. Buster scrambled up the steps ahead of Billy and his friends.

The platform was empty. A shutter covered the ticket window, and a bare lightbulb lit up the timetable posted next to it.

"It's just like I thought," Billy said, peering at the neatly printed schedule. "The last train of the day was supposed to be the local, at four thirty-seven."

"Well, *someone* must know about the train we saw," Dannie said. She was already heading through the door that led into the lodge. "Stay here, Buster," she said.

By the time Finn and Billy caught up to her, Dannie was at the ticket office inside. Someone was always there, even when the outside window was closed. Tonight it was a small, gray-haired man who wore glasses and a vest. He smiled at Dannie in a grandfatherly way.

"Sure I saw that train, little lady," he told her. "You'd have to be blind and deaf to miss it."

"What kind of train was it?" Finn asked as he and Billy hurried up next to Dannie. "Why wasn't it on the schedule?"

The old man peered at the boys over the top of his glasses. "I'm sorry, sonny," he said. "But I can't tell you that."

"Why not?" Billy asked. "Can't you just—"

"Billy!" a stern voice spoke up behind them.

Billy turned to see his father standing there in his wool suit and work boots. Mr. Cole's arms were crossed.

"Haven't I warned you not to bother folks when they're working?" he said.

"But, Dad!" Billy said. "We were just trying to find out—"

"No excuses," Mr. Cole said firmly. "It's late. Your mother must be wondering where you are. Go on home, all of you."

Billy knew better than to argue with his father. "Yes sir," he said. He turned and walked back outside behind Dannie and Finn.

"At least we know for sure that the train we saw *wasn't* on the schedule," Finn said as they started toward the family cabins. "Just like the electric storm in the message."

"But that train already came and went," Dannie pointed out. "The message makes it sound like the plan is for something that didn't happen yet. There's going to be a signal."

Billy walked silently, thinking about the pistol and the message. What did it all mean?

A few minutes later they crossed the footbridge to the clearing where the cabins were. Billy saw no sign of Eddie, Wes, or Jim.

"William Edmund Cole!" a voice called out.

Billy's cabin stood at the edge of the clearing, next to the footpath. Lights were on inside. Billy saw his mother frowning out at him through the open living room window.

"You come home this instant!" she said. "And bring Finn and Dannie with you."

"Uh-oh," Finn murmured.

The front door swung open. Billy's five-year-old sister, Marjorie, stood in the doorway. Her nightgown swayed around her as she hopped from one bare foot to the other.

"You're in trouble!" she whispered. "Everyone's been waiting and waiting."

Billy gulped when he saw all the people crowded into their tiny living room. Alice Ann, Janet, and Lucy sat cross-legged on the floor. They had changed out of their bathing costumes. Swollen spots on their faces and arms were covered with some kind of cream. They were a funny sight, but Billy didn't dare laugh. Not with the girls' mothers hovering over them like watchdogs.

Standing nearby were Billy's mother and Finn's mom, Mrs. Mackenzie. Dannie's father was there, too. Mr. Renwick stood off to the side, looking ill at ease in his faded work clothes.

Every person in the room was looking straight at Billy, Finn, and Dannie.

And there wasn't a single smiling face among them.

Chapter Five

UNFAIR!

"Can't you work any faster, Billy?" Alice Ann said the next afternoon.

Billy pushed a mop along the floorboards of the Lockharts' kitchen. He could see Alice Ann through the open doorway to the living room. She sat on the sofa, holding her embroidery hoop and needle. The smug look on her face made Billy scowl.

"Can't you find anything better to do than pester me all day long?" he shot back.

"Mother says I need to get my rest while these stings heal up," Alice Ann told him. She measured a length of red thread and cut it with scissors. "I promised I would make sure you do every chore you're supposed to. You're just lucky Mother's busy with the washing. She'd get awful steamed to see you moving so slow."

Billy wanted to get his chores done fast, too. But all kinds of questions kept crowding into his mind and distracting him. Questions about the pistol and who-ever had taken it from him. And about the mysterious message and what it might mean. Billy had tried to talk to his mother about them. But after hearing about the wasps' nest, she hadn't been in any mood to listen.

"Hey, Alice Ann," he said. "Did you hear anything about an electric storm?" he asked. "One that might hit without warning?"

Alice Ann was the biggest busybody in the camp. She always heard *everything.*

She glanced out the window at the bright sunshine. "A storm? On a day like today?" She gave Billy a funny look. "Besides, how could anyone know about it if there's no warning?"

Billy reached into the pocket of his knickers. His fingers touched the folded paper message, but he stopped himself from showing it to Alice Ann. She was such a busybody, she would probably tell everyone in Scenic.

"I guess you couldn't," he mumbled.

But he couldn't stop himself from opening his mouth again.

"What about the train that came through last night? It wasn't on the schedule. And the man in the ticket office wouldn't tell us a thing about it," he said. "Don't you think that's strange?"

As soon as he asked the question, Billy regretted it. Alice Ann straightened up, glaring at him.

"Well, *I* didn't see any train. Thanks to you, my eyes were nearly swollen shut from these stings," she said. "And I don't see what a train has to do with any storm, Billy Cole. You're just trying to get out of doing your chores! Now you keep mopping, or I'll tell Mother."

Billy opened his mouth to argue, then shut it again. "All right, all right. I'm mopping," he mumbled.

By the time Billy finished, it was nearly supper time. He put the mop and bucket away just as Alice Ann's mother brought in clean sheets from the line outside.

"I filled the coal bin and washed all the windows," he told her. "I mopped the kitchen floor, too, like you said to."

"That's fine, Billy," said Mrs. Lockhart. "You may go now."

He headed for the door like a shot. "Thanks, Mrs. Lockhart!" he said.

Just before the door closed behind him, he heard Alice Ann call out, "See you at rehearsal tomorrow. *All* afternoon."

Billy groaned. Did she have to remind him?

Finn and Dannie were sitting on the steps of Finn's cabin across the clearing. Buster was asleep in the shade beneath the steps. Billy knew they had spent the day doing chores, too, for the Kleigs and the Grinnells.

"It isn't fair!" Billy said as he came up. He dropped down on the bottom step next to Dannie. "Having Alice Ann boss me around all day was bad enough. And we couldn't do anything to find out more about that note. Do we really have to be in that dumb Fourth of July pageant, too?"

"You heard our parents," Dannie sighed. "They figure the only way we'll stay out of trouble is if we keep busy with the pageant."

Finn shrugged, kicking at the pine needles on the ground. "So much for being able to do whatever we want all summer," he said. "We even have to drop out of the war."

Billy heard a door slam shut. Wes, Eddie, and Jim were just coming out of the Gundys' cabin, next to Finn's. All three of them snickered.

"I guess that means you *lose* the war then," Eddie said, walking over to Billy and his friends.

"You're the ones that got beat last night!" Finn said hotly. "We got away before you knew what hit you!"

"We could have gotten you back," Jim said. "But we didn't need to. Not after what happened to Bil—"

"Let's go," Eddie said gruffly. He cut Jim off, steering him away from Finn's cabin.

"Wait!" Billy called out. "How do you know what happened? Did you see who put that sack over my head?"

Jim and Eddie kept walking. They didn't say anything more. Wes trailed behind, glancing down at his feet.

"What did you see, Wes?" Billy prodded. He lowered his voice. "Did you see the pistol?"

Wes's eyes shifted nervously. "I've gotta go," he mumbled. He ran after his brother and Jim.

Finn stared after the boys. "They saw what happened. They must have!" he said.

"If they did, then why didn't they help you, Billy? Why won't they talk about it?" Dannie asked.

"Knock-knock," Finn said.

Billy and Dannie looked at each other. "Who's there?" they both said at the same time.

"May," Finn told them.

"May who?" Billy asked.

"*May*be we should see what Philip thinks of all this," Finn said. "After all, his father is one of the railroad owners. If there's some kind of secret plan, maybe Mr. Mackey and Philip know about it."

* * *

Philip was the only kid in Scenic who didn't live in the family cabins. He and his father were just going to be in Scenic for a few months while Mr. Mackey, one of the owners of the railroad, saw to some business. They had taken up rooms in the old lodge. That was fine with Billy. There was always a feeling of excitement at the lodge—of important work going on.

Today was no different. Men were bustling around in the post office, telegraph room, barbershop, and security office on the first floor. Ernie Oliver, the young man who ran the store, waved to Billy, Finn, and Dannie as they dashed to the staircase. Upstairs, Billy saw that the door to his father's office was closed. Billy ran past without stopping. He and his friends raced down the long hallway to a door at the very end.

The door to the Mackeys' suite was half open. Billy saw Philip in the parlor room, standing in front of a mirror. Philip spoke to his reflection in a clear, deep voice.

"'We hold these truths to be self-evident, that *all* men are created equal...'" he recited.

"Oh, brother!" Finn muttered.

Philip whirled around. "Well, I have to learn my part for the pageant, don't I? I'm Thomas Jefferson!" he said. He dropped down on the sofa. "I heard about you being stuck in the pageant, too. I tried to tell Alice

Ann you weren't *trying* to hurt her. But she wouldn't listen."

Dannie rolled her eyes. "We didn't come to talk about that," she said.

She, Billy, and Finn all spoke at once, telling Philip what had happened the night before. When Billy got to the part about finding the burlap sack, Philip's eyes nearly popped out of his head.

"There was a *pistol* in it?" Philip said. "And you found a note?"

Billy pulled the message from his pocket and showed it to Philip. "Maybe you can help us figure it out. Seems like there's some kind of plan having to do with the railway. Have you heard your father say anything?" he asked.

Philip read the note, then shook his head. "Father hasn't said a word about any electric storm. Or about a signal," he said. Then he snapped his fingers. "What about Mr. Woods? Did you talk to him? If anyone knows about signals, he does."

"Sure! A telegraph operator sends and receives signals over the telegraph wire all the time," Billy said, nodding. "Why didn't I think of it before?"

"We saw Mr. Woods last night, too. Right before Billy found the pistol," Finn added. He plopped down on the overstuffed couch. "Do you think he could be mixed up in a plan to make the railroad company pay?"

Dannie shrugged. "Let's go talk to him," she said. She jumped up and headed for the door. Billy held back.

"Dad won't like it if he hears I'm bothering people at their work again," he said.

"Don't worry about that," Philip told him. "I go see Mr. Woods all the time when Father's busy working. Mr. Woods doesn't mind. He's even teaching me to play cards."

Billy didn't say anything. Because Mr. Mackey was one of the owners of the Great Northern Railway, most people in Scenic tended to let Philip have his way.

"All right," Billy said finally. "Let's go!"

The telegraph room was behind the stairs on the first floor of the lodge. As they walked down the back hall, Billy heard voices inside.

"That's three games in a row you've won, Trevor," said a man's voice. "I give up."

Billy heard the slap of cards against a table.

"Looks like today's my day to win big," said a second man. This time, Billy recognized the quick, eager voice. It was Mr. Woods. "Ready for another game?"

"Might as well," a third man spoke up. "I sure can't work my shift on the mucking crew anymore. Ever since the accident, my foot is useless. It's all the railway's fault!"

The man's bitter tone made Billy stop in his tracks. Finn, Dannie, and Philip paused, too. Inside the room, Mr. Woods said something Billy couldn't hear. Then the angry man spoke again.

"The company owes me!" he burst out. "And I'm going to make sure the goat pays up."

Billy, Dannie, and Finn looked at one another.

"'The goat will pay,'" Dannie whispered. "That's what it said in the message Billy found!"

CHAPTER SIX
ANGRY WORDS

Maybe that man's going to cause trouble for the railway!" Finn whispered.

Billy nodded. "I guess Mr. Woods isn't the only one we need to talk to."

Dannie pushed past the boys and stormed into the telegraph room. "What do you mean, Mister?" Billy heard her say. "Are you threatening the railway?"

Billy, Finn, and Philip crowded through the doorway behind her. Billy had never been in the telegraph room before. It was bare except for a couple of tables and chairs. The boxlike telegraph machine sat on a small table against the back wall. Cards and half-empty glasses of water were scattered across a larger table, in the center of the room. Mr. Woods and three other men sat around it.

Dannie was scowling at the man closest to the door. He didn't look much older than Billy's father, but he had a shiny, bald head. His right leg was stretched out straight, and a bandage covered his foot. A cane was hooked over the back of his chair. His brows were very bushy, and beneath them his dark eyes flashed with annoyance.

"Didn't your mama teach you any manners, young lady?" he said to Dannie. "My little girl wouldn't dare give a grown man your kind of sass."

No doubt about it, thought Billy. He was the man they'd heard talking about making the goat pay. Now, if they could just find out whether he had anything to do with the mysterious message....

"My mama's dead," Dannie said bluntly. "But I know she'd want me to stand up to folks who make no-good threats! What are you planning to do to the railway?"

"Now, hold on!" Mr. Woods cut in. He frowned across the table at Billy, Dannie, Finn, and Philip. "What do you kids think you're doing? You can't just barge in here making accusations."

"They came with me," Philip spoke up. "My friends, um, want to learn how to play cards, too. Can you teach them, Mr. Woods?"

Billy knew Philip was just making up an excuse so they could find out what Mr. Woods knew about the message. The blond man drummed his fingers against the cards on the table.

"Why don't you come back later?" he said, still frowning. Billy had the definite feeling he didn't want them there.

"But what about that message?" Dannie blurted out. She planted her hands on her hips, turning from Mr. Woods to the bald man. "What do you know about an electric storm that's not on a schedule?" she demanded. "What kind of plan are you going to signal?"

Finn shot a worried look at Billy. Had Dannie said too much? After all, they didn't have any kind of proof that Trevor or the other man had anything to do with the message they had found.

For a moment, Mr. Woods just stared at Dannie. Then he chuckled and said, "Can't say I get many telegrams about the weather. Unless it's some kind of storm that's causing damage. And that's mostly winter blizzards."

The young man ran a hand through his slicked-back hair. "The telegraph is for *big* news," he went on. "Like when that Commander Byrd fellow flew over the North

Pole last month. Or important railroad business from Seattle or Chicago. No one's going to waste their nickel to send word of a little rain."

Just then, the telegraph machine began to click and hum.

Tap-tap-tap-tap-tap.

The metal keys typed out a message on a slender paper tape. Billy stepped closer to look at it, but Mr. Woods waved him back.

"It's official railway business," he said. "If you kids want to learn about cards, you'll have to come back another time."

Billy could see that Mr. Woods hadn't been fooled by Philip's story. He quickly scanned the room.

Hmm. No sign of a burlap sack, Billy thought. *Or a pistol.*

He didn't dare stay any longer, though. Not with Mr. Woods watching him. As he stepped out the door, Billy glanced back at the bald man. The grouchy frown had never left his face.

"Gee whiz!" Finn whispered once they were outside in the hall. "Mr. Woods sure did want to get rid of us. Maybe he is mixed up in some kind of plan with that other fellow."

"You think he was just pretending not to know anything?" Philip asked. He shoved his hands into the pockets of his knickers.

"Dunno," said Billy. He started down the hall to the front of the lodge. "But he sure does like to talk big. Big progress, big news, big railroad business. Big, big, big!"

Dannie frowned. "Well, thanks to all his big talk, we couldn't learn a thing about that bald man's threat," she said. "We couldn't even find out his name!"

"His name's Pete Delray," Philip told them.

Finn, Dannie, and Billy turned to stare at him.

"He got hurt in an accident inside the tunnel," Philip went on. "A boulder broke loose and hit his foot. He lost a couple of toes, I think. He was talking about it over at the schoolhouse."

"The schoolhouse? What was he doing there?" Dannie asked.

"Well, he can't work on the mucking crew with a hurt foot. So he's been helping Miss Wrigley and Mrs. Lockhart with the scenery for the pageant," Philip explained. "I heard him tell Mrs. Lockhart he's afraid the railway might fire him now that his foot's no good. He sounded pretty mad."

"Maybe he has a plan to get back at the railway for his hurt foot," Billy said. "But if he's got a plan, he's not in it alone. Whoever wrote that note meant for someone *else* to get it," Dannie pointed out.

Finn pulled open the lodge doors and stepped onto the porch. Holding on to the railing, he looked out at the sun-drenched mountainside. "Well, I guess there's one good thing about being in the pageant," he said. "We'll be able to keep an eye on Pete Delray."

* * *

"Hurry up, or we'll be late!" Marjorie said the next morning.

Billy's little sister skipped ahead on the path that followed along the Tye River. It twisted through the woods, leading to the schoolhouse. Every so often, Marjorie turned to wait for Billy, Finn, and Dannie.

"Come on!" she squealed.

Billy rolled his eyes. "The pageant is all Marjorie can talk about," he said to Dannie and Finn. "Mother said she could be in it, too, since we'll be there to watch after her."

"Well, *I'll* be watching Pete Delray," said Dannie. "If he's got some kind of plan to hurt the railway, I'm going to find out what it is." She bent down to pick up a stick. "Here, boy!" she called.

Buster came scrambling from behind a thick clump of fir trees. Dannie let him sniff the stick, then threw it as far as she could. "Go fetch it, Buster!"

Her dog raced ahead and scrambled over the top of a ridge ahead of them. Billy and his friends climbed up a moment later. From the top, they could see the schoolhouse and groups of boys and girls in the yard, talking or playing hopscotch or marbles. Billy saw Alice Ann, Lucy, and Janet sitting on the rail fence. Philip stood next to them. He said something, and the girls all laughed.

"Hey!" Finn said. He pointed beyond the school. The mountainside rose up sharply. Lookout Rock, a wide, rocky ledge, stuck out from the bushy trees that covered the steep slope. "Isn't that Wes and Eddie?"

Billy saw two stocky figures moving on top of Lookout Rock. "It's them, all right. But that's not all," he said. "See what they're carrying?"

A burlap sack was slung over Eddie's shoulder. Billy was sure he saw something bulging at the bottom of it.

Something about the same size as a pistol.

Chapter Seven
SPOILED PLANS

Dannie let out a low whistle. "How'd they get *that?*"

"I don't know. But those Gundys sure have a lot of explaining to do," said Billy. "Let's go!"

He ran ahead on the path. Finn and Dannie were right behind him. He heard their lunch pails banging against their legs. Billy shot past Marjorie as she skipped into the school yard.

"Where are you going, Billy?" she asked.

"Never mind that," he called back to her. "Just stay here!"

Heads turned to stare. Billy paid no attention. He, Finn, and Dannie flew toward Lookout Rock.

"I can't see Wes and Eddie anymore," said Finn. He glanced up at the rocky ledge, shading his eyes from the sun. "They must be on their way up to—"

"Billy, Daniella, and Finn!" called a voice Billy knew only too well.

It belonged to their teacher, Miss Wrigley.

Billy turned around. Sure enough, Miss Wrigley stood at the top of the schoolhouse steps. She waved them back toward the yard.

"Please join the rest of the group," she told them. "Rehearsal is about to begin."

"Now?" Finn shot a frustrated glance up the rocky mountainside.

"Yes," Miss Wrigley said. She raised an eyebrow. "Unless your punishment has been lifted since your parents spoke to me yesterday?"

Billy kicked at the ground, frowning. "No, ma'am. We're coming," he said.

"Me, too!" Marjorie piped up. She rushed up the steps and tugged at Miss Wrigley's dress. "Did Mother speak to you about me being in the pageant too?"

"Why, yes, she did," said their teacher. She smiled warmly at Marjorie. "Mrs. Lockhart and I have a very important part for you to play...."

Marjorie skipped inside, beaming. The other children followed. Voices and laughter spilled out the windows of the two-room schoolhouse. Miss Wrigley was waiting for them, but Billy hesitated. He stared hard into the trees above Lookout Rock.

Wes and Eddie were up there somewhere. Billy just knew they had a pistol in that sack! If only he could find out what they planned to do with it....

"Children!" Miss Wrigley called.

With a sigh, Billy followed Finn and Dannie to the schoolhouse. They stopped in the coatroom to put away their lunch pails. Through the doorway Billy saw Miss Wrigley's classroom, where younger students were taught when school was in session. Now the room looked completely different. Desks had been pushed aside, leaving the center of the room open. Boys and girls stood reciting lines. Mrs. Kleig, Mrs. Gundy, and some other ladies from the camp sat at the desks along the wall. They were piecing together scraps of fabric into old-fashioned skirts, aprons, and caps. Miss Wrigley and Mrs. Lockhart hustled around, giving everyone instructions.

"Billy, look!" Marjorie squealed from the second classroom. "I'm helping!"

Billy turned to gaze into the other classroom, where Mr. Farnam taught Scenic's older boys and girls during the school year. After classes ended he had left Scenic for the summer. Now his classroom was filled with scenery and decorations. Cans of paint stood dripping onto old newspapers. Half-finished flags and eagles and crepe paper garlands were scattered about. Marjorie stood near the door. She held a paintbrush that dripped with brown paint.

"I'm making crates of tea for the Boston Tea Party!" she said excitedly. She swabbed paint across a wooden box that sat on the floor. More paint got on her jumper than on the box, Billy noticed. "How's this, Mr. Delray?"

Only then did Billy notice the bald man behind Marjorie. Pete Delray limped out from behind some boards that leaned against a desk. Leaning on his cane, he made his way over to Billy's little sister.

"That's just fine," he said. Mr. Delray smiled down at her, chuckling. "You are a topnotch helper, Marjorie."

Billy was surprised by the warmth in his face. Then Mr. Delray looked up and saw Billy, Dannie, and Finn. The smile disappeared. Marjorie didn't seem to notice.

"See, Billy? I'm going to help paint *all* the boxes," she went on. "Isn't that right, Mr. Delray?"

Pete didn't answer right away. He took a watch from the pocket of his trousers and glanced at it.

"Hmm? Sure. That's right," he said.

He patted the top of Marjorie's head distractedly. Then he turned and limped over to some older boys who were hammering a frame together for scenery.

Leaning on his good leg, Pete looked at his watch again. Billy heard one of the boys ask Pete a question three times before he answered.

"Why does Mr. Delray keep checking the time?" Finn wondered.

Billy shrugged. "Beats me." He saw Miss Wrigley making a beeline for them.

"You three should be in the other room," she said. "Rehearsal is already starting. Billy, you and Finn will be colonists who take part in the Boston Tea Party. And Daniella..."

"Yes?" Dannie said, through clenched teeth. Billy knew she hated it when their teacher called her by her full name. No matter how many times she asked, Miss Wrigley refused to call her Dannie.

"I'm afraid the female roles are already taken," Miss Wrigley told her. "Mrs. Lockhart and I had to put our heads together to find something suitable."

While she spoke, Miss Wrigley guided them into the other classroom. Alice Ann stood in front of the blackboard, tapping her foot impatiently. "Dannie! Where have you been? If you're going to play the part of my maid, you could at least be here to practice your lines when you're supposed to," she said.

"Oh, no," Dannie said, stopping short. "Don't tell

me I'm going to be Betsy Ross's *maid.*"

Their teacher gave a pleased nod. "Alice Ann will help you learn the part, Daniella. Just do whatever she says, and you'll be fine," she said.

"You mean, Alice Ann gets to boss me around?" Dannie said. She looked as if she had just swallowed a mouthful of dirt. "I have to *let* her?"

"Run along," Miss Wrigley said brightly. She gave Dannie a gentle push, then turned to Billy and Finn. "Now! Let's see if we can find some costumes for you two...."

Miss Wrigley kept the boys busy for the rest of the morning. First she had Mrs. Lockhart and Mrs. Gundy poke and prod them to measure for costumes. Then she made them go over their lines with some of the bigger boys. Billy and Finn didn't have a single chance to check on Mr. Delray.

At the end of the morning Dannie came over to the desks where Billy and Finn were practicing their parts. "I'm going to kill that Alice Ann!" she whispered. "I only have three lines to say in the pageant. Alice Ann must have made me repeat them a thousand times! I know she did it just to bother me."

Dannie sat down on one of the desktops. Her feet hung over the side. "Where's Mr. Delray?" she asked.

Before Billy could answer, Alice Ann appeared next

to them. "The other girls are waiting for you, Dannie," Alice Ann said. "Mrs. Gundy is going to teach us to make lace collars for our costumes."

Billy saw that the girls were all seated at desks against the opposite wall. Miss Wrigley and Wes's mother sat at the center of the group. Dannie took one look at them and shook her head.

"Not me," she said firmly. "I don't know how to do needlework. And I want to keep it that way!"

Alice Ann pressed her lips together. "Miss Wrigley! Dannie won't do what you've asked," she called.

"Just give it a try, Daniella," said Miss Wrigley. She gave Dannie an encouraging smile. "Mrs. Gundy has brought us some lovely silk thread to work with."

"Oh, goody," Dannie said flatly. Shoulders sagging, she followed Alice Ann over to the group. She grimaced as Mrs. Gundy helped her tie some shiny yellow thread onto a crochet hook.

"Let's get out of here," Finn said under his breath to Billy. "Quick, before Miss Wrigley makes *us* learn how to make lace, too!"

As soon as they reached the coatroom, Billy looked into Mr. Farnam's classroom. The first person he saw was Marjorie. She was playing patty-cake—with Mr. Delray. The man was laughing, and his eyes twinkled with merriment.

"You sure do remind me of my little Teresa Rose," Pete was saying. "She and her mama stayed back in Tacoma..."

Billy stood listening. Mr. Delray seemed like a different person from the frowning man they'd met in the telegraph room.

"He sure doesn't look like he's up to anything suspicious now," he whispered to Finn.

Mr. Delray looked up and saw them. He frowned. Finn tiptoed toward the door, gesturing for Billy to follow.

"He can't hear us here," Finn said when they got outside. "Just 'cause he's nice to Marjorie doesn't mean he's not planning to do something to the railway."

"I guess we just have to keep a closer eye on him," Billy said.

At that moment a sound rang out, making Billy jump. About a half mile up the mountain, warblers burst from the trees in a startled cloud.

"Cripes!" Finn cried. "Billy, someone just shot off a pistol!"

Chapter Eight

GUNSHOT ON THE MOUNTAIN

Billy swallowed hard. "That was Wes and Eddie. It had to be!" he said.

Finn ran down the steps and jumped over the school yard fence. By the time Billy caught up to him, he was halfway up the steep path to Lookout Rock.

"Wait, Finn! Miss Wrigley's going to notice we're gone," he said. "Then we'll *really* be in hot water."

Finn climbed the rest of the way up the rock. He strode past the pine-branch walls of a fort they had made a few months earlier. "We can't just sit here and do nothing," he insisted.

"Well..." Billy glanced nervously back at the schoolhouse. "Okay. But let's hurry!"

He scrambled up the path behind Finn. "Those birds flew out over there," he said. "Up by Crystal Lake, I'd say."

Finn turned just enough so Billy saw his nod.

The boys had been up the old Indian trail more times than Billy could count. His feet seemed to know just where to find a solid hold among the roots, rocks, and ferns.

"I don't get it," he said after a while. "I'm almost sure the person who got the sack and pistol away from me was bigger than Wes and Eddie. So how come they have it now?"

"I guess they'll have to tell us when we catch up to them," Finn said in a determined voice.

He pointed to a twisted fir tree, a landmark he and Billy recognized. A big patch of bark had been scratched clean off by a bear. Crystal Lake wasn't far off now.

Billy was alert for any movement. Every time he heard a rustle in the woods, he turned to peer into the trees. Squirrels and chipmunks scampered along pine branches. A snowshoe hare disappeared behind a rock with a flick of its tail. Billy listened carefully, but he didn't hear voices or footsteps. Just the gurgling of the Tye River running along the trail.

"Over there!" Finn said suddenly. He stopped and pointed across the river. "Wes! Eddie!" he shouted.

Billy spotted a big boulder through the trees. The Gundy brothers were standing on top of it. As they turned toward Finn and Billy, Billy saw a shiny pistol in Eddie's hand.

In the next instant, Eddie had grabbed the burlap sack from the ground. Billy saw him drop the pistol inside. A moment later, Eddie and Wes disappeared over the far side of the boulder.

"Hey! They're running away!" Billy said.

He and Finn took off in chase. They splashed across the river, soaking their boots and knickers up to the knees.

"They're heading back toward camp!" Finn said. He cut down and across the mountain at an angle, pushing past prickly pine branches.

Billy caught sight of Wes and Eddie up ahead. Wes's red shirt was a bright blur among the trees. Keeping his eyes on it, Billy ran faster. Branches slapped against his face. Rocks skittered out from beneath his soggy boots. Twice he stumbled. Still, he and Finn were gaining on the Gundys.

"Stop!" Billy shouted breathlessly.

Wes and Eddie didn't even slow down. They ran over the top of a ridge and out of sight.

"This way!" Finn said. He darted left, angling around the rocky ridge. "We'll cut 'em off farther down."

Billy followed, breathing hard. He slid down around

the steep side of the ridge. Cascading pebbles made it hard to keep his footing. His hands scraped against the sharp granite.

"Whoa!" Billy cried as his boots slipped out from under him. He slid to the foot of the ridge on the seat of his knickers, landing with a thump.

"Jeepers, Finn! What are you trying to do, get us killed?" he said.

Finn didn't answer. He stood in front of Billy as still as a statue.

"Billy, don't move," Finn whispered.

"Huh?" Billy looked up—and froze.

There, not ten feet in front of them, a bear stood scratching at the roots of a tree.

"A grizzly!" Billy breathed.

The bear's shaggy brown head reached only to about Billy's waist. "It's just a cub," he said.

Finn's eyes darted nervously around. "The thing is," he whispered, "cubs never stray very far from their mothers...."

Just then, Billy heard branches snapping on the far side of the tree where the baby bear stood.

"Oh, no," he said, jumping to his feet.

A huge grizzly bear came lumbering around the side of the tree.

Its beady eyes were fixed right on Billy and Finn!

CHAPTER NINE

GRIZZLY!

Fear shot through Billy like lightning. "What do we do now?" he squeaked out. He'd never seen a grizzly up close before. It was enormous—as big and bulky as one of the railcars that carried workers in and out of the tunnel. Billy gasped as the shaggy animal reared up on its hind legs. Razor-sharp claws three inches long waved in the air.

"Don't make any sudden moves," Finn whispered. "She'll chase us down for sure."

"What!?" Billy was trembling like a leaf. "She's going to charge, Finn!"

Finn shook his head ever so slightly. When he spoke, it was in a quiet, calm voice. "No, she won't. Not if we keep our heads," he said. "Back away, one step at a time. Go slowly."

Billy didn't think he could make himself budge—not with that huge grizzly so close to them. The cub at her side kept scratching at the tree roots. It ignored Billy and Finn completely.

Finn took a single step back. Billy breathed deeply, then did the same. He squeezed his eyes shut, waiting for the grizzly to charge.

"Keep going!" Finn whispered.

Opening one eye, Billy saw that the mother grizzly hadn't moved. "Nice bear," he murmured, taking another step back.

He wasn't sure how they managed it. Step by step, inch by inch, they moved farther and farther away. They kept up their slow, steady pace until they were well out of sight of the bears. Then they turned on their heels and ran as fast as they could. They didn't stop until they reached the Tye River. Billy collapsed on the rocky bank, gasping for air.

"That...was...close!" he said.

Finn gave a shiver. "My dad shot a grizzly once when he was hunting," he said. "He told me what to do in case I ever ran into one."

"Lucky for us," Billy said. Lying on his back, he stared up at the blue sky above the treetops. "Well, I guess we won't catch up with Wes and Eddie now."

* * *

"Where *were* you?" Dannie demanded when Billy and Finn got back to the school yard.

It was lunchtime. Boys and girls sat in groups on the steps or beneath the trees by the river. Dannie, Marjorie, and Philip sat together at the top of the riverbank. Buster lay next to them, gnawing on a bone. Billy's stomach growled when he saw boiled ham and bread in the pail his mother had prepared for him and Marjorie. He grabbed a slice of the thick, buttered bread and crammed it into his mouth.

"We went after Wes and Eddie," Finn explained. "They had the pistol, all right. They even shot it!"

"A pistol?" Marjorie asked. She stared at Finn with wide, curious eyes. "Were you playing cowboys and Indians?"

"Um, something like that," Billy said quickly. He shot a warning glance at his friends. They had to watch what they said around Marjorie. She was sure to blab every word to his parents.

"Say, Marjorie, why don't you go see if your pal Mr. Delray needs some more help?" Finn suggested.

Marjorie chewed a mouthful of ham and swallowed. "How can I do that?" she said. "He's not even here."

"He's not?" Billy blinked, surprised. He looked at Dannie and Finn, but they just shrugged.

"Someone came looking for Mr. Delray," Philip told them. "A man wearing a coverall. I saw them head toward camp about ten minutes ago."

Billy didn't like the sound of that. Not one bit. "What if that man gave Mr. Delray a signal?" he said. "A signal that it's time to make the goat pay. They could be doing something to hurt the railroad company right now!"

"You take that back!" Marjorie said. "Mr. Delray wouldn't hurt the railway. He's my friend!" She stuck out her lower lip in a stubborn pout.

"Listen, Marjorie—" Billy began.

Before he could say anything more, a bell rang from the schoolhouse. Billy saw Miss Wrigley standing in the doorway.

"Let's continue, children!" she called. "Colonists, we need you inside to practice the Boston Tea Party...."

The next hour seemed to drag on forever. Billy nearly jumped out of his skin with impatience. Philip had to remind him of his lines half a dozen times. But at last Miss Wrigley and Mrs. Lockhart announced that they were finished for the day.

"Come on! We need to find Mr. Delray," Billy said.

He pulled Dannie and Finn toward the door. He forgot all about Marjorie—until she yanked on his shirttail, pulling it loose from his knickers.

"Where are you going, Billy?" she asked.

"We, um..." Billy searched his mind for an excuse. His little sister stamped her foot.

"If you do anything to bother Mr. Delray, I'll tell Mother!" she said. "He's *not* going to hurt the railway!"

Billy glanced nervously around. Mrs. Gundy was hustling past them. But she didn't seem to have heard Marjorie. "Colin! There you are," she said, stepping right past Billy.

Billy was surprised to hear a deep voice speak up right behind him.

"Hello, sis."

Billy whirled around to see a short, stocky man. The man's eyes flickered toward Billy and Marjorie. Then he turned to Mrs. Gundy. "I brought you the rest of the silk," he told her. He handed over a basket filled with balls of soft, shiny yellow thread.

The man's stocky build was just like Wes and Eddie's. He was their uncle, Billy realized. The one Wes had talked about playing marbles with.

"Thank you, Colin," Mrs. Gundy said, taking the

thread. "Would you be a dear and help us with one more thing? We could use some strong hands to carry costume materials to the Recreation Hall. The Scenic Ladies Society is due to meet there at three o'clock."

"Can I go?" Marjorie asked Billy. "All the girls are going to help make costumes for the pageant."

She smiled at Lucy and Janet, who were getting their lunch pails. Janet raised an eyebrow at Dannie.

"Well, not *all* the girls," she said.

"Oh, brother," mumbled Dannie.

Billy was just glad they didn't have to worry about Marjorie tagging along with them. "Sure, you can go with Lucy and Janet," he told her. "Have fun."

Billy saw Philip at the back of Miss Wrigley's classroom talking to Alice Ann. It would take time to get him—and Billy didn't want to waste a second.

He, Finn, and Dannie stepped around Mrs. Gundy and Colin and slipped outside. Buster was sitting next to the schoolhouse steps. He wagged his tail happily as Dannie petted him. "Come on, Buster. We've got to find Mr. Delray. Fast!"

"Let's try the new tunnel," Finn suggested. "If he wants to get back at the railway for his injury, he might do something there."

They practically flew across camp. But when they

reached the tunnel, the lanky foreman of the work crew stopped them.

"Hold on there!" he said. "The tunnel is off-limits to kids. You know that."

"We're looking for someone," Finn told him. "Mr. Delray. He's got a hurt foot. Have you seen him?"

Billy gazed at the tunnel entrance. A dozen cars sat on the rails outside. Men used diesel shovels to unload blasted rock from the cars. It was noisy, grimy work, but Billy saw no sign of anything suspicious.

"Delray? There's no one by that name on my shift," the foreman said, speaking loudly above the noise.

"Maybe he snuck in," Dannie suggested.

The foreman shook his head firmly. "I keep a close eye on everything that goes on. I would have seen someone with a bandaged foot."

"Thanks anyway," Billy said. He shrugged at Finn and Dannie. They walked back toward camp.

Finn glanced nervously around at the bunkhouses, sheds, barns, and machines. "Gee whiz. There must be fifty buildings in camp," he said. "Maybe more. Mr. Delray could be in any one of them!"

"What about the lodge?" Dannie said. "There are lots of offices there. Mr. Delray might try to harm something there."

"Or some*one.*" Billy shivered, thinking of his father and Mr. Mackey and all the other people who worked in the lodge. "We'd better go look."

They ran back down the gravel road. A porch wrapped around one side of the lodge and shaded the front doors. "Stay here," Dannie told her dog. Then she went up the front steps to the porch. As Billy followed, he saw something move in the shadows along the side of the lodge. He walked toward it—and gasped.

"It's *him!*" Billy said. "Mr. Delray! And he's not alone."

Dannie and Finn ran up behind him. Billy pointed toward the end of the porch. A staircase there rose up to a small balcony on the second floor. Pete Delray was just stepping onto the stairs. A dark-haired man wearing a denim coverall was with him. They held something between them. It looked like some kind of pole, but Billy couldn't see it clearly.

"Don't those stairs go up to your dad's office, Billy?" Finn asked.

"Yep," said Billy. He kept staring at the long object Pete and the other man were carrying.

What is *it?* he wondered.

The two men reached a turn in the stairs and stepped through a patch of sunlight. The bright rays shone on the metal in their hands so that Billy could finally see what it was.

"They've got a drill bit!" he breathed.

It wasn't just any drill bit, either. It was from the enormous ring drills that were used inside the tunnel. The bit was ten feet long, at least.

Billy gulped when he saw the deadly point at its tip.

CHAPTER TEN
CHASING TROUBLE

Billy! They're taking that thing right to your dad's office," said Dannie. "What if they...?"

"They're not going to hurt my father," Billy cut in. "I won't let them!"

He whirled on his heel and raced for the front doors. "This way!" he said. "We'll take the inside stairs. Maybe we can get to Dad's office first and warn him!"

Billy moved faster than he ever had in his life. He, Finn, and Dannie tore through the front room where the ticket office was. Their boots made such a clatter on the stairs that Mr. Oliver called out from the store, "Hey, stop that racket!"

Billy just ran faster. As he neared the top of the stairs, he saw the door to his father's office. He raced down the hall toward it.

"Dad!" he cried, throwing the door open. It hit the wall with a bang that shook the whole room. Billy's father and Mr. Mackey were bent over some papers on Mr. Cole's desk. They whirled around in alarm.

"What's the matter, son?" asked Mr. Cole.

"Look out!" Finn said, charging into the office so fast he slammed into the desk. Papers and plans went flying. "Some men are coming! They want to—"

He gasped as the wooden door to the balcony creaked on its hinges. The door swung inward. Billy saw the point of the drill bit, and then the bald top of Pete Delray's head.

"You leave my dad and Mr. Mackey alone!" he yelled.

Billy flung himself against the door with all his strength. It banged against Mr. Delray and the drill bit. They were squeezed tight between the balcony door and the doorframe.

"*Ow!*" cried Mr. Delray.

The drill bit dropped from his hands. It banged heavily to the floor, half in and half out of the office. Billy couldn't see the other man. But he heard him out on the balcony, talking urgently to Mr. Delray.

"What's going on here?" said Mr. Mackey. Usually he was a laughing, loud man. But now his voice was tense. He and Mr. Cole pulled Billy away from the door.

"Billy, stop this instant!" said Mr. Cole.

Billy struggled to pull free, but his father kept a tight grip on his shoulders. Pete Delray stepped through the balcony door, the other man right behind him. Billy gasped as they bent to pick up the lancelike drill bit.

"But, Dad! Mr. Delray wants to get back at the railway for his hurt foot. With that!" Billy twisted around his father to point at the drill bit.

Dannie and Finn stood uncertainly next to Mr. Cole's desk, eyeing the drill bit warily. "Should I run to the security office and get Mr. Jenkins?" Dannie asked.

For a moment, Billy's father just stared at Billy, Finn, and Dannie. When he finally spoke, his voice was filled with disbelief—and annoyance.

"Do you mean to say," he said slowly, "that you're causing this ruckus because you think these gentlemen want to *hurt* Mr. Mackey and me? They're not here to do any harm. Mr. Delray and Mr. Fritz are here about a job!"

"Can't a fellow learn to work in the machine shop without you kids meddling?" Mr. Delray gave a disgruntled shake of his head.

Billy blinked as their words sank in. "A job? In the machine shop?" he repeated.

"That's right, kid," said the man Billy's father had called Mr. Fritz. He and Mr. Delray rested the sharp end of the drill bit on Billy's father's desk. "I've been training Pete myself," Mr. Fritz went on. "Thought I'd bring up a sample of his work to show you. It's good. And I could use the help."

"I can't work in the tunnel anymore," Mr. Delray added. He nodded at his bandaged right foot. "Not with this. But I can handle the sharpening machines just fine."

Billy only half-listened to the men. He felt more confused than ever.

"So...you didn't write any note about making the goat pay?" he asked.

Pete Delray stared blankly at Billy.

"You kids are talking riddles," Mr. Mackey said in his booming voice. He clapped Billy around the shoulders. "Why don't you run along and play? Your dad and I have important work to do."

Philip's father steered Billy toward the door. It was only then that Billy noticed Trevor Woods. He stood just outside the office. His eager eyes seemed to take in every detail—the flustered faces, drill bit, and scattered papers.

"Here's a telegram for you, Mr. Mackey," he said.

He handed over a strip of paper with a message typed on it. Then he asked, "Everything all right in here?"

"Fine," Mr. Cole answered. But he wasn't smiling. "Billy, you heard Mr. Mackey. You and your friends had better run along. And I don't want to hear any more about you bothering my workmen."

* * *

"Knock-knock," Billy said.

"Who's there?" Dannie asked.

They were on their way down the steps to the first floor of the lodge. "Shirley," Billy told her.

"Shirley who?" said Finn.

Trevor Woods was a few steps ahead of them. Billy lowered his voice and said, "Shirley do wonder who wrote that note I found. If it wasn't Mr. Delray, then who *was* it?"

"You're sure it wasn't Wes or Eddie?" asked Dannie. "They *did* have that pistol in a burlap sack. I bet anything it was the same pistol you found under the lodge, Billy."

Dannie made sense. But Billy felt certain the person who had thrown the sack over his head was a grown man, not a boy. "Wes and Eddie were up to something they didn't want us to know about, all right. But why would *they* have a plan to make the goat pay? They're just kids," he said.

He jumped lightly down the last few stairs, then waited for his friends. "Anyhow, we still don't know what the electric storm means," he added. "The one that's not on a schedule."

"No one would tell us about that train that wasn't on the schedule, either," Finn reminded him. He turned to look down the back hall that led to the telegraph room. "Mr. Woods?" he called out.

The blond man stopped just outside the door to the telegraph room. He glanced over his shoulder at Finn, raising an eyebrow. "I know you kids wouldn't ask me about any railway business," he said. "Not after Mr. Cole and Mr. Mackey just told you not to."

Had Mr. Woods heard them talking? Billy couldn't tell.

"I guess not," Finn answered with a sigh. "Never mind, Mr. Woods."

The three friends started toward the family cabins. Billy kept thinking about the mysterious message. Who was going to make the goat pay? And how?

The questions stayed on his mind even after he said good-bye to Finn and Dannie and headed to his cabin.

"Mother?" he called out as he stepped through the door.

Then he remembered. She was at the Ladies Society tea in the recreation hall. A plate of cookies sat on the table in the kitchen. Billy grabbed three, then climbed the steep stairs to the attic loft where he and Marjorie slept. His bed stood under a tiny window beneath the sharply slanted roof. Billy dropped down onto it. He felt beneath the mattress for the cigar box he kept there. Inside, lying on top of his garnets, was the note he had found inside the sack with the pistol. Billy read it for what seemed like the thousandth time.

"'Electric storm not on schedule. Wait for my signal. The goat will pay,'" he murmured.

He stared out the window, mulling over the words. What did they mean? If only he could find out...

A flash of red across the clearing caught his eye. It was Wes Gundy's shirt. Wes was bent over a pile of pine branches outside the Gundys' cabin, looking beneath them. Then he walked slowly around the cabin, bending every so often to peer underneath.

What's he looking for? Billy wondered.

He dropped the cigar box and was outside in less than ten seconds. As the cabin door banged shut behind him, Wes glanced up. When he saw Billy, his whole body stiffened. In the next instant, he turned on his heel and ran away.

"Not again," Billy said, groaning. He took off after Wes, kicking up pine needles. "You're *not* getting away," he said under his breath. "Not this time."

Wes was already racing across the footbridge that led to the main part of camp. Billy saw him cut behind the lodge.

"Oh, no you don't..." Billy muttered.

He was after Wes in a flash. Billy reached the back of the lodge just in time to see Wes clamber onto the raised wooden walkway that led to the recreation hall. In a flash, Billy climbed onto it, too.

Thump-thump-thump-thump... Wes's boots pounded on the wooden boards. But Billy was gaining fast. By the time Wes opened the door to the recreation hall, Billy caught up to him.

He grabbed hold of Wes's shirt. "You'd better tell me what you're up to, Wes Gundy!" he said, taking gulping breaths of mountain air.

"Try and make me!" Wes shot back. Twisting free, he ran inside the hall.

Billy tore after him. He caught a glimpse of tea cups, cakes, and costumes. He was vaguely aware of the ladies and girls at the tables, talking and sewing.

"Boys, *please!*" Mrs. Lockhart's shocked voice exclaimed.

Billy made a diving leap for Wes. He grabbed him around the waist, and they both fell to the floor.

Crash!

They hit one of the tables, knocking it over. Shrieks echoed through the hall. Billy heard his mother and Marjorie shouting his name, but he didn't stop. He and Wes pummeled each other as they rolled across the floor. Chairs and tables crashed over around them. They battled their way across the entire hall before Mrs. Gundy's brother finally pulled them apart.

"That's enough!" Colin said.

Chest heaving, Billy looked past Wes's scowling face. Half a dozen tables and chairs were overturned. A few cups and a teapot lay broken on the floor. Bits of smashed cake and puddles of tea were everywhere.

"Just look at what you boys have done," scolded Billy's mother, her face flushed with anger. She picked up an old-fashioned three-cornered hat that was ripped and covered with tea and cake. "Everything is ruined!"

Chapter Eleven
A Sneaky Plan

It took Wes and Billy nearly two hours to clean up the mess they had made in the recreation hall. And that was *after* the scolding their mothers gave them. By the time they finished, it was nearly supper time.

"You boys about ready to leave?" Wes's uncle Colin called out.

Colin was the only one left with them in the recreation hall. Their mothers and the other ladies and girls had left long before, taking the damaged costumes with them.

"Be right there," Wes called from behind the stage. He and Billy were putting their mops and buckets away in the back corner.

"So what are you up to, Wes?" Billy whispered. It was the first chance he had had to talk to Wes away from his uncle. "I saw you and Eddie with that pistol. Why'd you run away from Finn and me?"

Wes's eyes flickered moodily. "Leave me alone," he muttered.

"People who sneak around with pistols are up to no good," Billy said. "You and Eddie are cooking up some kind of plan. I know you are!"

He shot a quick glance toward the front of the hall. Wes's uncle leaned against the wall near the door, tossing his hat in his hands.

"You listen to me, Wes Gundy," Billy went on. "If you're thinking of using that pistol to hurt the railway, you'd better think again. I won't let you!"

Wes's mouth clamped into a tight line. "For your information, I don't have any pistol!" he said angrily. "But you knew that already. If anyone knows about pistols, it's you, Billy Cole!"

Billy blinked, surprised. What was Wes talking about? Why was he acting as if *Billy* had done something wrong?

"Why would *I* know about any pistols?" he asked.

Wes just glowered at him. He turned and jumped off the stage.

"I'm ready to leave, Uncle Colin," he said.

Colin hadn't said much while the boys were cleaning

up. But every so often Billy had caught Wes's uncle watching him. He glanced at Billy again just before he and Wes left the recreation hall.

It probably doesn't mean anything, Billy thought.

Still, Wes and Eddie were up to something. And one way or another, Billy was going to find out exactly what it was.

* * *

"You mean, we're going to sneak into their cabin?" Dannie said the next morning.

"Shhh!" Finn warned. "Not so loud."

He, Dannie, and Billy sat on a tree stump at the edge of the clearing near the family cabins. Buster sniffed at their lunch pails in the grass. Every so often he lifted his head to glance at boys and girls passing by on their way to the schoolhouse.

Alice Ann stuck her nose in the air as she and Janet walked past. "Hmph!" she sniffed. Billy could see she hadn't forgiven him for ruining the costumes at the Ladies Society tea. He did feel badly about the hard work wasted, even if it was only for the pageant. But he didn't have time to worry any more about that. He had important things on his mind.

"Maybe Wes and Eddie hid the pistol at home somewhere," Billy said, once Alice Ann and Janet were out of earshot. "Maybe we'll find something to help us figure out what they're up to. Or what that message means."

Finn pushed himself off the stump. "Well, now's our chance to look," he said. "Mr. Gundy's on shift inside the tunnel. And Mrs. Gundy is helping with the pageant at the schoolhouse."

"I even got Lucy to take Marjorie to the schoolhouse so she wouldn't tag along with us," Billy added. "If we're quick, Miss Wrigley and Mrs. Lockhart might not even notice we're late for practicing the pageant."

"Look!" Dannie pointed across the clearing at the Gundys' cabin. Wes and Eddie were just walking out the door. A few moments later, they disappeared inside Jim Walsh's cabin, halfway around the clearing.

Dannie and Finn jumped down from the tree stump to join Finn. The three of them circled around behind the cabins to the Gundys'.

"You keep watch, Buster," Dannie said as they tiptoed up the steps. "Stay."

The dog sat obediently on the crabgrass in front of the cabin. Billy took a deep breath. Then he slipped through the door behind Finn and Dannie. Right away his heart started to beat faster.

"If Mother and Dad ever find out we came here without permission—"

"We'll just have to make sure they *don't,* that's all," Finn cut in.

Billy took a few steps into the parlor and looked around. The Gundys' cabin layout was exactly like Billy's. There was a bedroom off the side of the parlor and a kitchen at the back. Stairs in the kitchen rose to the sleeping attic above.

"This place is as neat as a pin," whispered Dannie. She glanced at the sofa, table, and chairs in the parlor. A basket on the floor held torn, tea-stained clothes and flags for the pageant. "There's nothing here but some sewing."

"I'll check the attic," Finn said. "That's where Wes and Eddie sleep. Maybe they hid the pistol there." He disappeared into the kitchen. Billy heard him clomp up the stairs. He started to follow, then stopped.

"Hey, what's this?" he murmured.

A desk stood in a corner of the parlor. Letters, books, and papers were arranged neatly on it. A ball of shiny yellow thread sat at the center of the desk.

"Oh, brother. It's that awful silk thread," Dannie said, rolling her eyes.

But it wasn't the thread that had caught Billy's attention. It was the piece of paper that lay beneath it.

"Look!" he said softly.

Dannie peered over his shoulder at the words scrawled on the paper. "'Here's a little souvenir from the silk trains, sis. Fresh off the ship from China. Love, Colin,'" she read out loud. She shrugged.

"It's a note from Wes's uncle," she said. "So?"

"*So*...look at this!" Billy reached into the pocket of his knickers. He pulled out the slip of paper he had taken from his cigar box that morning, the message he'd found in the burlap sack with the pistol.

Billy unfolded the paper and laid it next to the note from Wes's uncle. "Notice anything?" he asked.

Dannie's eyes flickered back and forth between the two notes.

"Jiminy!" she said. "The handwriting is exactly the same!"

Chapter Twelve
FOLLOWING CLUES

A windstorm of questions swirled inside Billy's head.

"*Wes's uncle* wrote about the electric storm and the signal!" he said. He waved the message under Dannie's nose. "That must mean he's the one who..."

Billy broke off talking. He heard Finn's pounding steps on the attic stairs. Finn burst into the parlor a moment later.

"Someone's coming!" he hissed. "Didn't you hear Buster?"

Sure enough, Buster's loud barking echoed from the cabin steps. Billy had been so busy looking at the notes that he hadn't heard it. He peeked out the parlor window—then ducked back out of sight.

"It's Wes and Eddie and Jim!" he whispered. "We can't go out the front. They'll see us for sure!"

"This way!" Dannie raced into the kitchen. A warm breeze blew in through the half-open window next to the kitchen table. Dannie shoved the window the rest of the way up. Climbing onto the table, she scrambled out and dropped to the ground. Billy heard boots on the cabin steps.

"Hurry!" he whispered as Finn climbed out behind Dannie.

"What's Buster doing here?" Eddie's voice came from just outside. "Stop that barking, you dumb dog."

Billy was halfway out the window when he heard the door open. Wes and Eddie were on their way in!

Billy quickly slid the rest of the way out. He fell to the ground with a thump, thankful for the thick layer of pine needles on the ground. They cushioned his landing so he barely made a sound.

He started to get to his feet, but Finn grabbed his arm, pointing up at the window. Billy got the message. He sat back on his heels against the cabin, listening.

"So where's the pistol now?" Jim Walsh's voice said from inside the Gundys' kitchen.

Billy could hardly believe their luck. The boys were talking about the pistol! He heard the clink of a glass. Then came the sound of running water.

"Don't know," Eddie said. "We hid the sack under

the branches outside. Right where Uncle Colin put it the other night. But it's sure not there now."

Dannie's eyes went wide. She opened her mouth, but Finn put a warning finger to his lips.

"I bet Billy and Finn took it. They *must* have," Jim was saying inside the Gundys' kitchen. "After they saw you with the pistol on the mountain."

Billy nodded to himself. Now he knew what Wes had been looking for around his cabin the day before. The pistol! Somehow it had disappeared.

"That's the last time I'll let Eddie talk me into something as crazy as shooting off a pistol," Wes muttered. "Especially one we're not even supposed to know about. Uncle Colin made us promise not to touch it, or tell anyone! Not even Mother or Father."

Billy crouched below the window, listening. He was more sure than ever that Colin was the one who had a plan to make the goat pay. He had written the note—and warned Wes and Eddie not to talk about the gun.

But what *was* the plan? Did Wes and Eddie know about it? What did their uncle need a pistol for? And where was he now?

"I don't know what you're so worried about," Eddie's voice came through the window. "Before Uncle Colin went back to Seattle we told him about the pistol being missing. He said to forget about it. So that's what I'm going to do."

Billy heard the boys' boots on the attic stairs. Their voices grew fainter. He couldn't make out their words anymore.

"Let's go," he mouthed to Finn and Dannie. Keeping close to the trees, they headed for the path that led to the schoolhouse. They didn't stop until they reached the stump where they had left their lunch pails.

"It sure looks like Wes and Eddie's uncle is mixed up in this," said Finn.

"I'll say. Finn, you should have seen the note Billy and I found!" Dannie exclaimed.

Finn scratched his head as they told him about the handwriting on the note. "Gee whiz," he said. "But...why would Mrs. Gundy's brother want to make the railway pay? He doesn't even live in Scenic, or work here, either."

Billy had been asking himself an even bigger question. "Who's got the gun now?" he wondered. "We don't have it, and neither do Wes and Eddie. And Colin's already left Scenic."

"Maybe he took it with him," Dannie suggested. But Billy didn't think so.

"Why would he bother to bring it here and hide it? Especially just to take it away again? Why wouldn't he just keep it with his things? It doesn't make sense," he said. "And you can bet Wes won't tell us anything about his uncle. He's about as talkative as a stone whenever he's around us."

"Well, maybe *Wes* won't talk to us," Dannie said with a sly smile. "But I know someone else who might."

With that, she picked up her lunch pail and started down the path toward the schoolhouse.

* * *

"Sorry we're late, Mrs. Gundy," Dannie said a few minutes later.

She, Billy, and Finn had just come running into the schoolhouse. Billy saw Philip and some other boys and girls in front of the blackboard. They were reenacting the signing of the Declaration of Independence. Mrs. Lockhart and Miss Wrigley hovered over them, giving directions and prompting them when they forgot their parts. Mrs. Gundy sat with a group of girls at the desks on one side of the classroom.

Billy saw that Lucy, Alice Ann, and Marjorie were among the group. They all held crochet hooks with shiny, yellow silk thread dangling from them.

"We're working on our lace collars 'til it's our turn to practice," Alice Ann said. She held up her crochet hook and made a face at Dannie. "But I don't suppose *you're* interested. I saw what a mess you made of the silk thread yesterday."

Dannie smiled sweetly—a little too sweetly. "I'd sure like to give it another try," she said. "Mrs. Gundy, could you show me again?"

Alice Ann's mouth fell open. Dannie ignored her. She sat down next to Wes's mother. Billy chuckled when he saw the look of fake interest on Dannie's face.

"I've never seen silk thread before," she went on. "Did you say that your brother gave it to you? That man who was here yesterday?"

Wes's mother had taken a small ball of the shiny thread from a pile on the desk in front of her. She turned to Dannie with a pleased smile. "Why, yes. Colin brought the thread. Isn't it lovely?" she said. "He found it in one of the railcars after his last trip east on the silk train."

"Silk train?" Dannie repeated. "What's that?"

Billy knew she was trying to learn more about Colin. But whatever Colin was planning, Billy doubted Mrs. Gundy knew about it. After all, Colin had made Wes and Eddie promise not to tell their parents about the pistol. Still, Mrs. Gundy might know *something* that could help them.

"Goodness! You don't know about the silks?" Mrs. Gundy said. As she spoke, she looped thread around the hook to make a chain of stitches for Dannie. "There are a few trains that travel on the Great Northern line, bringing silk from Seattle. Fast as they can get it off the boat from China, men load the silk onto the *Northern Lightning.* That's the name of the silk train Colin works on. He's a guard on the train. He rides with the silk clear across the country to the mills back east. That's where they make it into silk fabric...."

"Well, I've never even heard of the *Northern Light - ning,*" Alice Ann said indignantly. "Does it come through Scenic?"

"I've sure never seen it on the schedule at the depot," Lucy added.

"Billy..." Finn elbowed Billy in the side. But Billy was busy listening to Wes's mother.

"Oh, the silk trains don't run on any schedule," Mrs. Gundy was saying. "The railroad company keeps them a secret from most folks. With a valuable cargo like silk, you don't want people knowing every detail. Colin says there's always a chance that hoodlums might try to rob the *Northern Lightning,* even with him on board. The silk is worth millions, you know."

Dannie sat bolt upright. "Hey! What about the train

that came through a couple nights ago?" she said. "It wasn't on the schedule. Was *that* one of the silk trains?"

Mrs. Gundy smiled. "Why, yes! Not the *Northern Lightning*, mind you. Colin said the *Lightning* was in the yard for repairs. I guess one of the other trains went out instead."

"Billy!" Finn whispered urgently.

But Billy barely heard him. Mrs. Gundy's words echoed inside his head. "The *Northern Lightning*, huh?" he muttered. Then he snapped his fingers. "Finn! Lightning is the same thing as——"

"An electric storm! That's what I've been trying to tell you!" hissed Finn. "So the *Northern Lightning* must be the electric storm in the note you found. A storm that's not on any schedule. It's the silk train!"

"Jeepers!" Billy's mind raced a mile a minute. "And Mrs. Gundy's brother is a guard on the train. He's the one who wrote the note about how the goat is going to pay...."

Finn grabbed his arm. "There's something in the note about a signal, right?" he asked.

"Yup," Billy answered. He had memorized every word of the note. "'Wait for my signal.'"

"Don't you get it?" Finn said. "Most folks don't

know when a silk train will come through. But a guard who rides on the train *would* know. I bet Colin is planning to signal someone when the *Northern Lightning* is ready to leave Seattle!"

Billy nodded. "We thought there was a plan to make the goat pay by hurting my dad, or the tunnel, or something else here in camp," he said. "But that's not it at all. It's a plan to rob the silk train!"

Chapter Thirteen
SIGNAL FROM SEATTLE

We've got to tell someone!" Finn said. "A silk train could be coming through Scenic anytime. If hoodlums are planning to rob it, we've got do something to stop them."

"Yes," Billy agreed. "But we'd better be careful who we tell. We still don't know who Colin wrote that note to. He could be working with anyone in the whole camp!"

Billy saw that Dannie was looking over at him and Finn. A messy tangle of yellow thread dangled from her crochet hook. Dannie thrust it at Mrs. Gundy.

"I guess I'm not cut out to make lace after all, Mrs. Gundy. But thanks for trying to teach me!" Dannie stood up suddenly, squeezed out of the circle of girls, and ran over to Billy and Finn.

"Did you hear all that?" she whispered.

"Sure! Dannie, we figured out what the note means," Finn said.

He and Billy tripped over each other's words in their rush to share what they had guessed. Dannie kept nodding and nodding. "That's just what I think," she said. "The switchbacks above camp are the perfect place for a robbery. Trains have to go slow, and there's nothing but forest for miles around."

"All we have to do is figure out who Colin is working with," Billy said. "Who's he going to send the signal *to?*"

"Signal? What signal?" a voice spoke up right next to them.

Billy turned to see Philip standing there. The warm air inside the schoolhouse had made his cheeks red. He pushed his blond hair off his forehead, looking curiously at Billy, Finn, and Dannie.

"I saw you whispering the whole time I was practicing my lines," Philip said. "It's about that message you showed me, isn't it? Did you learn something more about Mr. Delray?"

Billy, Dannie, and Finn looked at each other. A lot had happened since they'd overheard Pete Delray's angry outburst about the railway in the telegraph room. "Can you keep a secret?" Finn asked.

Just then, Miss Wrigley clapped her hands at the front of the room. "Colonists! I need you up here to rehearse the Boston Tea Party...."

"Oh, brother," Billy mumbled. "How can we be stuck here? We should be trying to find the person who's going to rob the silk train!"

Philip's mouth dropped open, but Billy didn't have time to explain. Miss Wrigley and Mrs. Lockhart were already giving directions to him and Finn. As they took their places at the front of the classroom, Billy saw Philip and Dannie talking with their heads close together.

The rest of the morning dragged on so slowly Billy could hardly stand it. By the time they stopped for lunch, he was almost bursting with impatience. Finn, Dannie, and Philip started toward the riverbank with their lunch pails. Billy stepped in front of them, crossing his arms.

"We don't have time to sit around here," he said. "We've got to figure out who's waiting for Colin's signal about the *Northern Lightning!*"

"What about Mr. Delray?" Philip asked. "He sure wants to make the goat pay. We heard him say so."

Billy glanced at the schoolhouse steps where Pete Delray sat with Marjorie on his lap. She laughed delightedly as he gave her a cookie from his lunch pail.

"Dad thinks all Mr. Delray wants from the railway is a different kind of job," Billy said. "But I guess he could still be the person Colin is going to send a signal to."

"Hold on. There's something I don't get," said Dannie. She kicked at a tree root that stuck up from the pine needles. "How's Colin going to send a signal all the way from Seattle? He can't mail a letter. The *Northern Lightning* would be through Scenic and over the mountains before the letter even got here."

"He could ring up on the phone," Finn suggested. "Or maybe send a telegram."

There were only two telephones in Scenic, Billy knew. One was in his father's office. The other was in the security office. Both offices—and the telegraph room—were in the lodge.

"Come on!" Billy said, starting toward the main part of camp. "Let's see what we can find out."

They ran through the woods and past the family cabins. As they reached the main camp, Billy heard the muffled blast of dynamite deep inside the tunnel. Men clomped along the walkways between the bunkhouses, the cookhouse, and the lodge. Billy had to wait for three workers in coveralls to go through the front doors of the lodge. Then he, Finn, Dannie, and Philip ran inside.

"Mr. Jenkins?" Dannie called. She stopped next to the security office, across from the ticket office. But when she turned the knob and pulled, the door remained shut.

"He must be making rounds through the camp," Finn said. "Never mind. Let's try the telegraph room."

"I'll look for our fathers upstairs," Philip offered.

Billy was already running down the back hall. *Be care - ful,* he warned himself. Trevor Woods—or anyone else in Scenic—could be the person Colin was signaling about the silk train.

He stopped just outside the telegraph room. Taking a deep breath, he peeked through the doorway.

The office was empty. All was quiet—except for the squat black telegraph machine.

Tap-tap-tap-tap...

The message tape dangled over the side of the machine. It grew longer as the machine typed out a telegram. Finn ran past Billy to the machine. He held the tape, looking at it.

"It's for Mr. Mackey," he said. "From the railway office in Chicago. They want to know about the progress inside the tunnel."

Billy frowned. That didn't sound like anything having to do with the silk trains. "Hmm." He looked around. "Are there any other telegrams we can look at?"

Finn bent to look more closely at the tape. "Maybe so," he said. "Look. This isn't one tape, it's two!" He pointed to the slot where the message tape came out of the telegraph machine. "The top tape gets ripped off and delivered to whoever it's for. But the same message gets saved on the bottom tape, too. See?"

The bottom tape stretched to the back of the machine. There it was connected to something that looked like the wooden spools his mother kept in her sewing basket. But instead of thread, the telegraph tape was wrapped around it.

"Well, let's take a look," Billy said. He unwound some of the tape. He barely looked up as Philip hurried into the telegraph room.

"Father and Mr. Cole are inside the tunnel," Philip said.

Billy nodded, not really listening. He began to read the blurry typed words on the telegraph tape. Philip, Finn, and Dannie clustered around him.

"This one's for Ernie Oliver, over at the store. It's just a list of supplies that are coming in from Wenatchee," Billy said. "Then there's one for my dad about the payroll, and—hey! Look at this!"

"What?" asked Philip, leaning closer.

Billy held out the tape so they could read the telegram:

12:17 NORTHERN LIGHTNING LEAVING
SMITH COVE

"That's it!" Dannie exclaimed. "That's the signal!"

"Uh-oh," said Philip. He pointed at the clock that sat next to the telegraph machine. "It's nearly half past noon now!"

Billy felt a knot twist in his gut. "That means the silk train is already on its way here," he said. "Somebody's going to try to rob it. And we still don't know who it is!"

Chapter Fourteen
TOO LATE!

You mean we're too late?" Finn said. He banged his fist on the wall. "We can't be!"

Panic rose up inside Billy. He tried to fight it back so he could think clearly. "We've got to find Mr. Jenkins," he said. "And get word to my dad and Mr. Mackey inside the tunnel."

He started to run from the room, but Dannie stopped him. "There's something funny about this telegram," she said. "It doesn't say who it's for."

Billy whirled back around. When he looked at the tape, he saw that Dannie was right.

"Then how could Mr. Woods know who to deliver it to?" Philip wondered.

The answer hit Billy with the force of a round of dynamite.

"Mr. Woods didn't have to deliver it to anyone. The message is for him!" he said. "Mrs. Gundy's brother knew Mr. Woods would be the first one to see it, so he didn't put a name on it."

"That's why Mr. Woods isn't here," Dannie added. "He must be on his way to rob the train right now!"

A terrible silence fell over the room. Then Finn shook himself.

"We've got to stop him!" he said.

His voice spurred Billy into action. He ran from the telegraph room, down the hallway, and out the front doors of the lodge. He skidded to a stop at the railing. Shading his eyes with his hand, he peered along the winding road that rose up the mountainside toward Stevens Pass.

"I bet he went that way," Billy said, thinking out loud. "The road gets pretty close to the switchbacks in some spots. If we—"

"There he is!" Finn exclaimed. He grabbed Billy's arm and pointed the other way down the road. "See that truck?"

A dusty truck was backing out of a garage beyond the recreation hall. Billy recognized the round face and slicked-back hair of the man behind the wheel. "It's Mr. Woods, all right. How are we going to stop him? There's no time to get help!"

"Maybe there is," Philip said. Billy saw determination in his eyes. "But someone will have to follow Mr. Woods and make sure he doesn't do anything to the *Northern Lightning* before I bring help."

Dannie stared at him blankly. "But how can we…"

Philip didn't give her a chance to finish her question. He bolted down the lodge steps and out into the road. He stood there blocking Trevor Woods's truck.

"Mr. Woods!" Philip shouted, waving his arms. "Stop!"

"What's he doing?" Finn murmured. Billy shrugged.

Out on the road, Mr. Woods slowed the truck to a stop. "What in the world is going on, Philip?" he asked.

"Father is looking for you," Philip said. "He needs to send a telegram to Chicago. It's urgent!"

Billy knew Philip was making up the story. "He's trying to stop Mr. Woods," he whispered. "But I don't think it's working."

Trevor Woods was frowning. He drummed his fingers impatiently against the steering wheel. "I'm afraid no telegrams can go out right now," he said. "Line's down again…."

"That's a lie!" Dannie breathed. "The machine was working fine just a minute ago."

"Tell your father I'll send that message as soon as I

track down the break," Mr. Woods was saying. "Now, I really need to be going...."

Philip stayed in front of the truck. He glanced at Billy, Finn, and Dannie. Then he nodded slightly toward the open truck bed.

"Of course!" Billy whispered. "If we climb in back without Mr. Woods seeing, he'll take us right to where he's going. *That's* how we can make sure he doesn't rob the train before Philip gets help!"

"That sounds awful dangerous," Dannie said, biting her lip. "But it'll be worse if Mr. Woods gets away with stealing that silk. Let's go!"

The three of them ran along the porch to the side of the lodge. There, a small stairway went down to the road behind the truck. As they tiptoed down it, Billy heard Philip talking.

"You're sure you'll be back soon, Mr. Woods? Father doesn't like to be put off, you know...."

Billy chuckled to himself. When Philip had first arrived in camp, Billy had hated the way the railroad owner's son acted like a spoiled prince. But his royal attitude sure was coming in handy now! Finn and Dannie were already climbing into the truck bed. Billy joined them as fast as he could.

Please don't see us... he begged silently.

He was glad Philip kept on talking. Mr. Wood's answers were filled with impatience. Billy didn't think Philip would be able to delay him for much longer. He, Dannie, and Finn squeezed right up against the back of the closed cab. They ducked down as low as they could so Mr. Woods wouldn't see them through the truck's rear window.

Seconds later, Billy heard the grinding of gears. The truck jerked forward on the road. Billy braced his boots against the rattling truck bed to keep from being tossed around.

As they drove into the trees beyond camp, Billy saw Philip race toward the tunnel.

"I sure hope he's fast," Finn whispered.

Billy just nodded. He didn't dare speak—not with Trevor inside the truck cab a few feet away.

The gravel road gave way to rutted dirt tracks. The smells and sounds of camp faded away. Before long, all Billy saw were the fragrant evergreens that grew thickly on both sides of the road. Once, he spotted the rails of the switchbacks through the trees. But Mr. Woods didn't stop the truck. He kept right on driving, higher and higher up the mountain. Billy, Dannie, and Finn bounced and shook in the back of the truck bed until Billy's whole body felt numb and bruised.

Then, all at once, Mr. Woods cut the motor and the truck stopped.

Billy's whole body tensed. He and his friends ducked even lower in the truck bed.

Don't look back here. Please *don't look back here,* thought Billy.

He heard rustling inside the cab. Then the door of the truck opened with a loud creak. Billy held his breath. He heard Mr. Woods grunt. Then he heard the young man's footsteps as they moved off into the woods.

Billy, Finn, and Dannie waited until the sounds grew faint. Only then did they dare to peek over the side of the truck bed.

"He's heading toward the switchbacks," Dannie whispered.

Billy saw the gleaming rails through the trees. Mr. Woods was plodding in their direction. A bulging burlap sack was slung over his shoulder.

"Well, now we know who took the pistol after Wes and Eddie hid it near their cabin," Billy said under his breath. He climbed out of the truck as quietly as he could. "We'd better follow him."

Billy, Finn, and Dannie stayed a safe distance back, keeping close to the trees. Mr. Woods was heading toward the switchback, Billy saw. That was where the tracks stopped before zigzagging back the other way to rise higher up the mountain.

When Mr. Woods reached the switchback, he let the burlap sack drop to the ground. Then he pulled out a crowbar and a sledgehammer. He wedged the crowbar underneath one of the iron pins that held the tracks in place. Finally he swung the hammer high and brought it down against the crowbar.

Clang!

The noise echoed in the still mountain air.

"He's pulling the pins out," Finn said. "He's going to damage the track so the silk train can't get past!"

Billy frowned as Mr. Woods pulled the pin loose. Right away the man went to work on another pin. The sledgehammer came banging down over and over again.

"Jeepers!" Billy said softly. Then he heard something else.

The chugging of a train engine.

He turned around, peering down the mountainside. Puffs of smoke rose into the sky. They didn't look more than a quarter mile away. And they were getting closer.

Finn and Dannie saw them, too.

"Uh-oh," Finn said, gulping. "The *Northern Lightning* will be here any minute!"

Chapter Fifteen
No Time to Lose

Billy watched in horror as the silk train moved closer. And closer.

Bang! Bang! Bang!

Mr. Woods's sledgehammer beat against the iron rails. Billy saw him turn to look down the mountainside. He began to work even faster.

"He's got another pin out!" Dannie whispered.

Mr. Woods tossed the iron pin aside. Then he started to hammer at the rail itself.

"Uh-oh. He's going to move it out of line," Finn whispered.

Billy looked back in the direction of the road. There was no sign of Mr. Jenkins—or any other help on the way.

"We can't wait," he decided. "We've got to stop Mr. Woods now—or the *Northern Lightning* will go right off the tracks!"

"But *how* can we stop him?" Dannie eyed the shiny pistol that lay on the burlap sack next to Trevor.

"We'll have to take him by surprise, that's all," Finn whispered.

That's all? thought Billy. Fear rose up inside him. But when Finn began to circle around the trees behind Mr. Woods, Billy and Dannie followed right behind him.

Billy caught a glimpse of Mr. Woods and the switchback through the trees. *Good,* he thought. The rail was still in place. But he knew it was just a matter of time before Mr. Woods would succeed in banging it out of line. And the *Northern Lightning* was getting closer every second!

Billy could see the silk train now. It moved slowly toward them through the trees. The chugging of its engine was growing louder. Mr. Woods was so intent on his work that he didn't see Billy, Finn, and Dannie. They moved closer and closer behind him.

Finn bent to scoop up pinecones and sticks as he went. Billy understood right away what his friend was doing. This wasn't just a pretend war. This time, the enemy was real. They were going to need all the ammunition they could get. Billy nodded at Dannie, and the two of them began to collect more pinecones and sticks. Before long, they were just a dozen feet behind Mr. Woods. Finn turned to look over his shoulder at Billy and Dannie.

"Now!" he whispered.

The three of them shot from the trees. Mr. Wood straightened up in surprise. He whirled around, and his mouth fell open. "What the...?"

Billy hurled pinecones at Trevor as hard as he could.

"Hey!" Mr. Woods yelped as the first ones hit him. He dropped the sledgehammer and threw his hands in front of his face. A second later, Billy, Dannie, and Finn slammed into him. They knocked Mr. Woods straight off his feet.

The four of them went tumbling down the rocky slope below the switchback. Billy rolled head over heels amid an avalanche of dirt and rocks. He wasn't sure how far he fell before he hit a small sapling that stopped him.

"Finn! Dannie!" he cried as he scrambled to get to his feet.

He didn't see either of his friends. But he did see Trevor Woods. He lay sprawled in the dirt next to another tree a few feet away. As he pushed himself up,

Mr. Woods shot a panicked glance up the mountain. The train was just fifty yards from the switchback now. It was slowing to a crawl.

"I bet Mrs. Gundy's brother is just waiting for you to stop the train so you both can rob it," Billy said.

"Colin tried to warn you to back off," Mr. Woods said, over the noise from the engine. "You should have taken the hint, kid."

"Warn me? You mean when he threw that sack over my head?" Billy was so mad his chest heaved. "He left that pistol and note for *you!* But after he got the sack away from me, he had to hide it again somewhere else."

Mr. Woods took a step, then winced. He rubbed his left ankle. "I didn't know why the pistol wasn't where it was supposed to be. Not 'til I heard you three talking about seeing the Gundy boys with it," he said.

Billy thought back to the day before. "You must have heard us talking right after you delivered the telegram to Mr. Mackey in my dad's office," he said slowly. But there was something else he still didn't understand.

"How did you know Colin was going to send you a signal about the *Northern Lightning?*" Billy asked. "You couldn't have seen the note he put in the sack with the pistol. Because *I* took it."

Mr. Woods kept looking up the hill. The silk train

was just reaching the switchback. "Colin had already told me the name of the train. So today I recognized his signal even without the note," he said. "Maybe you stopped me from getting the pistol for a few days. But you're not going to stop me from getting that silk!"

Gritting his teeth, Mr. Woods began to hobble back up the slope. At that moment, Dannie and Finn jumped out from behind a tree just uphill from Billy.

Dannie held a long, bushy pine branch. She swung it at Mr. Woods, hitting him in the chest. He stumbled, then whirled angrily to face her.

"Why, you little punks..." he said.

"Hold it right there!" a deep voice called from the hill above.

Billy, Finn, Dannie, and Trevor whirled around. Billy's father, Mr. Mackey, Mr. Jenkins, and Philip were standing right next to the switchback. Mr. Woods's shiny pistol was in Mr. Cole's hand.

"We rang ahead to Wenatchee," Mr. Mackey called down. "Police are ready to pick up Colin as soon as the silk train gets there."

"Are you kids all right?" Billy's father asked.

Behind him, the *Northern Lightning* was just changing directions. With a blast of its whistle the train moved higher up the mountain. Billy smiled.

"We're fine," he called back to his dad.

"And so is the silk," Philip's father said. He turned to watch as the train picked up speed. "Thanks to you kids."

* * *

"Well now!" Cal Jenkins said later that afternoon. "I guess we're done here. You kids can go on home to your cabins now."

Billy, Finn, Dannie, and Philip had been stuck inside the security office ever since they'd returned to Scenic. Billy was sure they must have answered hundreds of questions. Maybe even thousands.

First, Cal Jenkins, Billy's father, and Mr. Mackey had wanted to hear every detail of what had happened over the last four days. Then Billy and his friends had to tell the story *again* to the man who came in the Skykomish police car to take Mr. Woods to the jail. When Billy finally stood up to leave, his legs were sweaty from sitting on the bench in the stuffy office.

"Your mother left word that she and Marjorie have gone for a swim. You'll find them at the river," said Billy's father. He put his arm around Billy's shoulders. "That was some quick thinking, son. I'm proud of you."

Billy didn't think he could stop grinning if he tried.

And that wasn't the end of the attention, either. When he, Finn, Dannie, and Philip got to the swimming hole, everyone crowded around them.

"Mr. Woods tried to rob the silk train?" Janet asked. "All by himself?"

Billy opened his mouth to answer, but his mother beat him to it. "He had a partner," Mrs. Cole said. She stood in the shallow water while Marjorie splashed at her feet. "All we need to know is that both men are safely in jail now."

Billy, Finn, Dannie, and Philip exchanged glances. They knew more of the story, of course. But Billy understood why his mother hadn't mentioned Colin's name. Wes and Eddie Gundy were at the swimming hole, too. They sat on the riverbank without saying a word. Billy guessed they felt pretty bad about their uncle. He didn't want to make it worse.

"Mr. Woods and his, um, partner told police that they were going to unload as much silk into the truck as they could. They planned to drive it across the border to Canada and then sell it," Billy explained.

Alice Ann pressed her lips together into a line. "How could they move all that silk?" she said.

"Well, they couldn't have taken all of it," Dannie said. "But a whole truckload of silk is worth thousands of dollars! Maybe even fifty thousand dollars."

A few boys whistled. That was more than most men earned in a whole lifetime.

"But why did he do it?" Lucy wondered out loud.

Finn shrugged. "The way Mr. Jenkins figures it, Mr. Woods wanted big things in his life. He just didn't want to work hard to get them. So he decided to rob the silk train for a quick payoff."

"Dad found out that Mr. Woods used to be the telegraph operator out at Smith Cove, in Seattle," Billy added. "That's where he met Co—" Billy just barely stopped himself from saying Colin's name. "That's where he met the other fellow. After Trevor got a job here in Scenic, they planned the robbery together."

Billy turned to see Miss Wrigley walking toward the swimming hole in her bathing costume and cap.

"I've just heard some lovely news," she said, stepping carefully down the bank to the water's edge. "Mrs. Lockhart and I were afraid we wouldn't have the costumes repaired in time for the pageant."

"Do you think we should call it off?" Dannie asked hopefully.

"Goodness, no!" Miss Wrigley told her. "There's no reason to. Especially since we've just gotten word from the company that owns the silk. They're so grateful to you children for stopping the robbery that they're sending us new costumes from New York City—made of silk! The pageant will go on as planned!"

Alice Ann and her friends cheered especially loudly. But all Billy could do was groan.

"Oh, brother!" he said.

He took hold of the rope that dangled in front of him. With a running start, he jumped out from the bank.

"Billy Cole, you wouldn't dare!" he heard Alice Ann shout.

Billy just grinned. Then he dropped into the water, splashing as hard as he could.

Author's Note

I got the idea for the *Cascade Mountain Railroad Mysteries* from a surprising place—a calendar! This calendar was made by my uncle, David Conroy, and was all about the building of the Cascade Tunnel. Until I saw it, I hadn't realized my grandfather was the general manager in charge of building the Cascade Tunnel. He brought his family—my Grandma Conroy, Uncle Dave, and my mom—to live in Scenic while the tunnel was being built. Grandpa Conroy saved lots of photographs, and my uncle used some of them in his calendar.

As soon as I saw the picture of children outside Scenic's two-room school house (my uncle is the rascal in the white shirt in the second row, third from the right), I wanted to know more. More about the tunnel. More about the Scenic camp. More about what it was like to be a kid in

Scenic back then. I started asking questions, and the result is *The Cascade Mountain Railroad Mysteries.*

The Cascade Mountain Railroad Mysteries are made-up stories, but I've tried to make the setting as much like the real Scenic as possible. The old ski lodge, the school house, and the family cabins were all part of the real camp. So was the swimming hole in the Tye River. The train tracks above Scenic really did zigzag back and forth in switchbacks like the ones shown in the map at the front of this book. Other sites were invented for the story. I simplified descriptions of the tunnel to keep the story from getting too complicated. Also, I must admit that the map of Scenic is entirely made up! After three-quarters of a century, it was impossible to know exactly where everything was, but I have tried to capture the spirit of the place.

Why the Railroad Needed a Tunnel

Before the eight-mile Cascade Tunnel was built, crossing the Cascade Mountains was dangerous— especially in the winter. Avalanches were a constant threat. The Great Northern Railroad tried to protect its trains by building wooden shelters over the tracks called snowsheds. But the snowsheds weren't always enough. In 1910, an avalanche swept two trains off the tracks and 150 feet down into a canyon. 101 people were killed.

A shorter tunnel, just 2.6 miles long, had already been built higher up the mountain. The Great Northern Railroad decided to build a new, longer tunnel lower on the mountainside, where snowslides were less of a danger. When the new Cascade Tunnel was finished in 1929, it was the longest tunnel in the United States. It is still one of the longest tunnels in the world today.

Diagram of Cascade Tunnel route

The Silk Trains

Silk made in China and Japan has been greatly prized by people all over the world for centuries. Raw silk—silk

yarn that hasn't yet been woven into cloth—is delicate and spoils easily, so it must be transported quickly and carefully. From the 1890s until around 1940, that important job was carried out in the United States and Canada by silk trains. Silk that arrived by ship at West Coast ports was carried across the country on special trains to silk mills on the East Coast.

An ancient Chinese painting on silk

The Silks, as the silk trains were called, were much faster than other trains of their day. They could go as fast as ninety miles an hour. They had priority over all

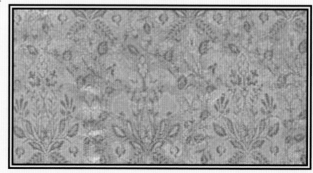

Expensive silk brocade

other rail traffic and stopped only for fuel and water. Once even the king of England had to wait while a silk train zoomed past!

Cars on silk trains were specially cushioned to minimize damage to the silk. Armed guards often traveled on board. That was because silk wasn't just delicate—it was also extremely valuable. A trainload of silk was worth as much as two and a half million dollars!

The 1930s were hard times for many Americans. Not many people could afford expensive silk clothes and silk stockings. In addition, silk producers in Asia found a cheaper way to get their silk to the East Coast—through the Panama Canal. Fewer and fewer silk trains traveled the railways. Gradually the silk trains vanished.

A silk moth lays eggs

Silk worm

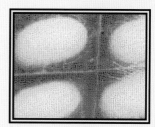

Silk worm cocoons

Raw silk from the cocoons

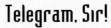

Telegraph
operator

Telegram, Sir!

In 1926, people didn't have cell phones, e-mail, satellite communications, or instant messaging. Telephone service was very expensive, especially for long distance calls. Mail service was much slower than it is today. People generally used the telegraph to send information quickly over long distances. Here's how telegrams—messages sent by telegraph—were sent:

☐ First the message was typed into a machine called a teleprinter.

☐ The teleprinter converted the message to a code called Morse code.

☐ The coded signals were then sent as pulses of electricity along a telegraph wire.

☐ When the message reached its destination, another teleprinter translated the coded signals back into words. Then it typed the message out onto a tape.

Telegraph service was used a lot in the 1920s. Reporters transmitted big news stories. Banks and companies sent records of stock trades and stock prices. Telegrams remained an important way of sending information through the 1960s.

Samuel F. B. Morse, inventor of the telegraph.

A costume party held in Scenic's community house

Showtime in Scenic

Men worked hard to build the Cascade Tunnel. But they also liked to have fun. The Great Northern Railway made sure there was always plenty of entertainment in the small work camp town. Moving pictures were shown twice a week. There were also boxing matches, basketball games, plays, dances, minstrel shows, banquets, and masquerade parties.

Special activities were arranged for the children of Scenic, too. They enjoyed visits from magicians, jugglers, and even a traveling portrait artist. Kids also had opportunities to show off their own talents. They put on shows for the adults in the recreation hall, much like the made-up Fourth of July pageant in this story.

A magic show

In 1926

◻ Bathing costumes were very different from the bathing suits worn today. Boys and girls alike wore suits that had a top and a bottom. A sleeveless top fell to below the hip and was worn over fitted shorts. Women also wore caps, stockings that came halfway to the knee, and special bathing shoes.

The author's mom in her bathing costume

◻ Dance crazes included the Charleston, the Black Bottom, the Shimmy, the Fox Trot, and the Tango.

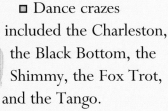

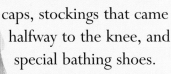
Dancing the Charleston

◻ Jazz music was hot! Some of the most popular jazz musicians of the day were Bessie Smith, Louis Armstrong, and Duke Ellington.

OCT. 27 AND 28
Circus poster

◻ A ticket to the circus cost about 75 cents. A double scoop ice-cream cone cost just 5 cents.

Louis "Satchmo" Armstrong, a great jazz trumpeter, composer, and movie star

About the Author

Anne Capeci has written many mysteries and other books for children, including titles in popular series such as *Wishbone Mysteries*, *Magic School Bus Science Chapter Books*, and *Mad Science*. She is also the author of CASCADE MOUNTAIN RAILROAD MYSTERIES BOOK 1: *Danger: Dynamite!* and BOOK 2: *Daredevils*. Anne lives in Brooklyn, New York, with her husband and two children.